The Lion of Petra

Talbot Mundy

Contents

CHAPTER I 7

CHAPTER II 20

CHAPTER III 30

CHAPTER IV 40

CHAPTER V 54

CHAPTER VI 64

CHAPTER VII 78

CHAPTER VIII 92

CHAPTER IX 102

CHAPTER X 109

CHAPTER XI 122

CHAPTER XII 132

CHAPTER XIII 142

THE LION OF PETRA

BY

Talbot Mundy

CHAPTER I

"Allah Makes All Things Easy!"

This isn't an animal story. No lions live at Petra nowadays, at any rate, no four-legged ones; none could have survived competition with the biped. Unquestionably there were tamer, gentler, less assertive lions there once, real yellow cats with no worse inconveniences for the casual stranger than teeth, claws, and appetites.

The Assyrian kings used to come and hunt near Petra, and brag about it afterward; after you have well discounted the lies they made their sculptors tell on huge stone monoliths when they got back home, they remain a pretty peppery line of potentates. But for imagination, self-esteem, ambition, gall, and picturesque depravity they were children--mere chickens--compared to the modern gentleman whom Grim and I met up with A.D. 1920.

You can't begin at the beginning of a tale like this, because its roots reach too far back into ancient history. If, on the other hand, you elect to start at the end and work backward the predicament confronts you that there wasn't any end, nor any in sight.

As long as the Lion of Petra has a desert all about him and a choice of caves, a camel within reach, and enough health to keep him feeling normal--never mind whose camel it is, nor what power claims to control the desert--there will be trouble for somebody and sport for him.

So, since it can have no end and no beginning, you might define this as an episode--a mere interval between pipes, as it were, in the amusing career of Ali Higg ben Jhebel ben Hashim, self-styled Lion of Petra, Lord of the Wells, Chief of the Chiefs of the Desert, and Beloved of the Prophet of Al-Islam; not forgetting, though, that his career was even supposed to amuse his victims or competitors. The fun is his, the fury other people's.

The beginning as concerns me was when I moved into quarters in Grim's mess in Jerusalem. As a civilian and a foreigner I could not have done that, of course, if it had been a real mess; but Grim, who gets fun out of side-stepping all regulations, had established a sort of semi-military boarding-house for junior officers who were tired of tents, and he was too high up in the Intelligence Department for anybody less than the administrator to interfere with him openly.

He did exactly as he pleased in that and a great many other matters--did things that no British-born officer would have dared do (because they are all crazy about precedent) but what they were all very glad to have Grim do, because he was a bally American, don't you know, and it was dashed convenient and all that. And Grim was a mighty good fellow, even if he did like syrup on his sausages.

The main point was that Grim was efficient. He delivered the goods. He was perfectly willing to quit at any time if they did not like his methods; and they did not want him to quit, because there is nothing on earth more convenient for men in charge of public affairs than to have a good man on their string who can be trusted to break all rules and use horse-sense on suitable occasion.

I had been in the mess about two days, I think, doing nothing except read Grim's books and learn Arabic, when I noticed signs of impending activity. Camel saddles began to be brought out from somewhere behind the scenes, carefully examined, and put away again. Far-sighted men with the desert smell on them, which is more subtly stirring and romantic than all other smells, kept coming in to squat on the rugs in the library and talk with Grim about desert trails, and water, and what tribal feuds were in full swing and which were in abeyance.

Then, about the fourth or fifth day, the best two camel saddles were thrown into a two-wheeled cart and sent off somewhere, along with a tent, camp-beds, canned goods, and all the usual paraphernalia a white man seems to need when he steps out of his cage into the wild.

I was reading when that happened, sitting in the arm-chair facing Grim, suppressing the impulse to ask questions, and trying to appear unaware that anything was going on. But it seemed to me that there was too much provision made for one man, even for a month, and I had hopes. However, Grim is an aggravating cuss when so disposed, and he kept me waiting until the creaking of the departing cart-wheels and the blunt bad language of the man who drove the mules could no longer be heard through the open window.

"Had enough excitement?" he asked me then.

"There's not enough to be had," said I, pretending to continue reading.

"Care to cut loose out of bounds?"

"Try me."

"The desert's no man's paradise this time o' year. Hotter than Billy-be- ----, and no cops looking after the traffic. They'll shoot a man for his shoe-leather."

"Any man can have my shoes when I can't use 'em."

"Heard of Petra?"

I nodded as casually as I could. Everybody who has been to Palestine has heard of that place, where an inaccessible city was carved by the ancients out of solid rock, only to be utterly forgotten for centuries until Burkhardt rediscovered it.

"Heard too much. I don't believe a word of it."

"There's a problem there to be straightened out," said Grim. "It's away and away beyond the British border; too far south for the Damascus government to reach; too far north for the king of Mecca; too far east for us; much too far west for the Mespot outfit. East of the sun and west of the moon you might say. There's a sheikh there by the name of Ali Higg. I'm off to tackle him. Care to come?"

"When do we start?"

"Now, from here. Tonight from Hebron. I'll give you time to make your will, write to your lady-love, and crawl out if you care to. Ali Higg is hot stuff. Suppose we leave it this way: I'll go on to Hebron. You think it over. You can overtake me at Hebron any time before tonight, and if you do, all right; but if second thoughts make you squeamish about crucifixion--they tell me that Ali Higg makes a specialty of that--I'll say you're wise to stay where you are. In any case I start from Hebron tonight. Suit yourself."

Any man in his senses would get squeamish about crucifixion if he sat long enough and thought about it. I hate to feel squeamish almost as much as I hate to sit and think, both being sure-fire ways of getting into trouble. The only safe thing I know is to follow opportunity and leave the man behind to do the worrying. More people die lingering, ghastly deaths in arm-chairs and in bed than anywhere.

So I spoke of squeamishness and second thoughts with all the scorn that a man can use who hasn't yet tasted the enmity of the desert and felt the fear of its loneliness; and Grim, who never wastes time arguing with folk who don't intend to be convinced, laughed and got up.

"You can't come along as a white man."

"Produce the tar and feathers then," said I.

"Have you forgotten your Hindustani?"

"Some of it."

"Think you can remember enough of it to deceive Arabs who never knew any at all?"

"Narayan Singh was flattering me about it the other day."

"I know he was," said Grim. "It was his suggestion we should take you with us."

That illustrates perfectly Grim's way of letting out information in driblets. Evidently he had considered taking me on this trip as long as three days ago. It was equally news to me that the enormous Sikh, Narayan Singh, had any use for me; I had always supposed that he had accepted me on sufferance for Grim's sake, and that in his heart he scorned me as a tenderfoot. You can no more dig beneath the subtlety of Sikh politeness than you can overbear his truculence, and it is only by results that you may know your friend and recognize your enemy.

Narayan Singh came in, and he did not permit any such weakness as a smile to escape him. When great things are being staged it is his peculiar delight to look wooden. Not even his alert brown eyes betrayed excitement. Like most Sikhs, he can stand looking straight in front of him and take in every detail of his surroundings; with his khaki sepoy uniform perfect down to the last crease, and his great black bristly beard groomed until it shone, he might have been ready for a dress parade.

"Is everything ready?" asked Grim.

"No, sahib. Suliman weeps."

"Spank him! What's the matter this time?"

"He has a friend. He demands to take the friend."

"What?" I said. "Is that little ---- coming?"

Two men in all Jerusalem, and only two that I knew of, had any kind of use for

Suliman, the eight-year-old left-over from the war whom Grim had adopted in a fashion, and used in a way that scandalized the missionaries. He and Narayan Singh took delight in the brat's iniquities, seeing precocious intelligence where other folk denounced hereditary vice. I had a scar on my thumb where the little beast had bitten me on one occasion when I did not dare yell or retaliate, and, along with the majority, I condemned him cordially.

"Who's his friend?" asked Grim.

"Abdullah."

Now Abdullah was worse than Suliman. He had no friends at all, anywhere, that anybody knew of. Possibly nine years old, he had picked up all the evil that a boy can learn behind the lines of a beaten Turkish army officered by Germans-- which is almost the absolute of evil--and had added that to natural depravity.

"Let Abdullah come," said Grim. "But beat Suliman first of all for weeping. Don't hit him with your hand, Narayan Singh, for that might hurt his feelings. Use a stick, and give him a grown man's beating."

"Atcha, sahib."

Two minutes later yells like a hungry bobcat's gave notice to whom it might concern that the Sikh was carrying out the letter of his orders. It was good music. Nevertheless, quite a little of the prospect was spoiled for me by the thought of keeping company with those two Jerusalem guttersnipes. I would have remonstrated, only for conviction, born of experience, that passengers shouldn't try to run the ship.

"What shall I pack?" I asked.

"Nothing," Grim answered. "Stick a toothbrush in your pocket. I've got soap, but you'll have small chance to use it."

"You said I can't go as a white man."

"True. We'll fix you up at Hebron. The Arabs have scads of proverbs," he answered, lighting a cigarette with a gesture peculiar to him at times when he is using words to hide his thoughts. "One of the best is: `Conceal thy tenets, thy treasure, and thy traveling.'

"The Hebron road is not the road to Petra. We're going to joy-ride in the wrong direction, and leave Jerusalem guessing."

Five minutes later Grim and I were on the back seat of a Ford car, bowling along the Hebron road under the glorious gray walls of Jerusalem; Narayan Singh and the two brats were enjoying our dust in another car behind us. There being no luggage there was nothing to excite passing curiosity, and we were not even envied by the officers condemned to dull routine work in the city.

Grim was all smiles now, as he always is when he can leave the alleged delights of civilization and meet life where he likes it--out of bounds. He was still wearing his major's uniform, which made him look matter-of-fact and almost commonplace--one of a pattern, as they stamp all armies. But have you seen a strong swimmer on his way to the beach--a man who feels himself already in the sea, so that his clothes are no more than a loose shell that he will cast off presently? Don't you know how you see the man stripped already, as he feels himself?

So it was with Grim that morning. Each time I looked away from him and glanced back it was a surprise to see the khaki uniform.

The country, that about a week ago had been carpeted with flowers from end to end, was all bone-dry already, and the naked hills stood sharp and shimmering in heat-haze; one minute you could see the edges of ribbed rock like glittering gray monsters' skeletons, and the next they were gone in the dazzle, or hidden behind a whirling cloud of dust. Up there, three thousand feet above sea-level, there was still some sweetness in the air, but whenever we looked down through a gap in the range toward the Dead Sea Valley we could watch the oven-heat ascending like fumes above a bed of white-hot charcoal.

"Some season for a picnic!" Grim commented, as cheerfully as if we were riding to a wedding. "You've time to crawl out yet. We cross that valley on the first leg, and that's merely a sample!"

But it's easy enough to be driven forward in comfort to a new experience, never mind what past years have taught, nor what imagination can depict; if that were not so no new battles would be fought, and women would refuse to restock the world with trouble's makings. A reasoning animal man may be, but he isn't often guided by his reason, and at that early stage in the proceedings you couldn't have argued me out of them with anything much less persuasive than brute force.

We rolled down the white road into Hebron in a cloud of dust before midday, and de Crespigny, the governor of the district, came out to greet us like old friends; for it was only a matter of weeks since he and we and some others had stood up to death together, and that tie has a way of binding closer than conventional associations do.

But there were other friends who were equally glad to see us. Seventeen men came out from the shadow of the governorate wall, and stood in line to shake hands--and that is a lengthy business, for it is bad manners to be the first to let go of an Arab's hand, so that tact is required as well as patience; but it was well worth while standing in the sun repeating the back-and-forth rigmarole of Arab greeting if that meant that Ali Baba and his sixteen sons and grandsons were to be our companions on the adventure. They followed us at last into the governorate, and sat down on the hall carpet with the air of men who know what fun the future holds.

Narayan Singh stayed out in the hall and looked them over. There is something in the make-up of the Sikh that, while it gives him to understand the strength and weaknesses of almost any alien race, yet constrains him more or less to the policeman's viewpoint. It isn't a moral viewpoint exactly; he doesn't invariably disapprove; but he isn't deceived as to the possibilities, and yields no jot or tittle of the upper hand if he can only once assume it. There was scant love lost between him and old Ali Baba.

"Nharak said, [1] O ye thieves!" he remarked, looking down into Ali Baba's mild old eyes.

Squatting in loose-flowing robes, princely bred, and almost saintly with his beautiful gray beard, the patriarch looked frail enough to be squashed under the Sikh's enormous thumb. But he wasn't much impressed.

"God give thee good sense, Sikh!" was the prompt answer.

"Fear Allah, and eschew infidelity while there is yet time!" boomed a man as big as the Sikh and a third as heavy again--Ali Baba's eldest son, a sunny-tempered rogue, as I knew from past experience.

"Whose husband have you put to shame by fathering those two brats?" asked a third man.

Mahommed that was, Ali Baba's youngest, who had saved Grim's life and mine at El-Kerak.

They all laughed uproariously at that jest, so Mahommed repeated it more pointedly, and the Sikh turned his back to consider the sunshine through the open

---

1 Greeting!

door and the rising heat within. Suliman and the other little gutter-snipe proceeded to make friends with the whole gang promptly, giving as good as they got in the way of repartee, and nearly starting a riot until Grim called Ali Baba into the dining-room, where de Crespigny was shaking up the second round of warm cocktails in a beer-bottle.

Ali Baba chose to presume that the mixture was intended for himself. The instant de Crespigny set the bottle on the table the old rascal tipped the lot into a tumbler and drank it off.

"It is good that the Koran says nothing against such stuff as this," he said, blinking as he set the glass down. "I have never tasted wine," he added righteously.

"Are the camels ready?" asked Grim.

"Surely."

"What sort are they? Mangy old louse-food, I suppose, that had been turned out by the Jews to die?"

"Allah! My sons have scoured Hebron for the best. Never were such camels! They are fit to make the pilgrimage to Mecca."

"I suppose that means that the rent to be charged for each old camel for a month is more than the purchase-price of a really good one?"

"The camels are mine, Jimgrim. I have bought them. Shall there be talk of renting between me and thee?"

"Not yet. After I've seen the beasts. If they're as good as you say I'll pay you at the government rate for them per month."

"Allah forbid! The camels are yours, Jimgrim. For me and mine there will no doubt be a profit from this venture without striking bargains between friends."

Grim smiled at that like a merchant listening to a salesman. It is not often that you can tell the color of his eyes, but on occasions of that sort they look iron-gray and match the bushy eyebrows. He turned to de Crespigny.

"Have you finished the census, 'Crep?"

"Pretty nearly."

"Have you got Ali Baba's property all listed?"

"Yes."

"And that of his sons and grandsons?"

"Every bit of it that's taxable."

"Good. You hear that, Ali Baba? Now listen to me, you old rascal. When you complained to me the other day that there was no more thieving left to do in Hebron, I told you you're rich enough to quit, and you admitted it, you remember? You agreed with me that jail isn't a dignified place for a man of your years and experience."

"Taib. [2] Jail is not good."

"But you complained that you couldn't keep your gang out of mischief."

"Truly. They are young. They have talent. Shall they sit still and grow fat like a pasha in the harem?"

"So I said I'd find them some honest employment from time to time."

"That was a good promise. Here already is employment. But you know, Jimgrim, they are used to rich profits in return for running risks. Danger is meat and drink to them."

"They shall have their fill this trip!" said Grim.

"Taib. But the reward should be proportionate."

"Government wages!" Grim answered firmly. The old Arab smiled.

"Under the Turks," he answered, "the officer pocketed the pay, and the men might help themselves."

"D'you take me for a Turk?" asked Grim.

"No, Jimgrim. I know you for a cunning contriver--an upsetter of calculations--but no Turk. Nevertheless, as I understand it, we go against Ali Higg, who calls himself the Lion of Petra. Sheikh Ali Higg has amassed a heap of plunder--hundreds of camels--merchandise taken from the caravans; that should be ours for the lifting. That is honest. That is reasonable."

"Not a bit of it!" said Grim. "Let's get that clear before we start. I know your game. You've got it all fixed up between yourselves to stick with me until Ali Higg is *mafish** and then bolt for the skyline with the plunder. Not a bit of use arguing--I know. You shouldn't talk your plans over in coffee-shop corners if you don't want me to hear of them."

--------- * Lit., nothing--corresponds to "na-poo" in Army slang. ---------

"Jimgrim, you are the devil!"

"Maybe. But let's understand each other. Your property in Hebron is all listed.

2 All right

We'll call that a pledge for good behavior. You and your men are going to have government rifles served out to you that you'll have to account for afterward. Every rifle missing when we get back, and every scrap of loot you lay your hands on, will be charged double against your Hebron property. On the other hand, if any camels die you shall be reimbursed. Is that clear?"

"Clear? A camel in the dark could understand it! But listen, Jimgrim."

The venerable sire of rogues went and sat crosslegged on the window-seat, evidently meaning to debate the point. If an Arab loves one thing more than a standing argument it is that same thing sitting down.

"We go against Ali Higg. That is no light matter. He will send his men against us, and that is no light matter either. They are heretics without hope of paradise and bent on seeing hell before their time! Surely they will come to loot our camp in the dark. Shall we not defend ourselves?"

But Grim was not disposed to stumble into any traps.

"Does a loaded camel on the level trouble about hills?" he asked.

But Ali Baba waved the question aside as irrelevant.

"They come. We defend ourselves. One, or maybe two, or even more of Ali Higg's scoundrels are slain. Behold a blood-feud! Jimgrim and his friends depart for El-Kudz[3] or elsewhere; Ali Baba and his sons have a feud on their hands.

"Now a feud, Jimgrim, has its price! It would do my old heart good to see the blood of Ali Higg and his heretics, for it is written that we should smite the heretic and spare not. But we should also despoil him of his goods, or the Prophet will not be pleased with us!"

"That is the talk of a rooster on a dung-hill," Grim answered. "A rooster crows a mile away. Another answers with a challenge, but the camels draw the plow in ten fields between them. That is like a blood-feud between you and Ali Higg. Five days' march from here to Petra and how many deserts and tribes between?"

"So much the easier to keep the loot when we have won it!" answered Ali Baba.

"There's going to be no loot!" said Grim.

"Allah!"

"Would you rather have me send back to Jerusalem for regular police?"

---

3 Jerusalem

"Nay, Jimgrim! That would be the end of you, for those police would bungle everything. You need clever fellows with you if you go to sup with Ali Higg."

"Well? Are you coming?"

"Taib. We are ready. But--"

"On my terms!"

"But the pay is nothing!"

"So is my pay nothing! This man"--he pointed to me--"gets no pay at all. Narayan Singh, the Sikh, gets less pay than a policeman."

"Then what is the profit?"

"For you? The honor of keeping your word. The privilege of making fair return for past immunity. Why aren't you and all your sons in jail this minute? Why did I invite you to come with me on this occasion? Because a man looks for friends where he has given favors! But if you consider you owe the administration nothing for forgiving all past offenses, very well; I'll look for friends elsewhere."

"As for the administration, Jimgrim, may Allah turn its face cold! But you are another matter. We will come with you."

"On my terms?"

"Taib."

You would have thought that settled it, especially as Ali Baba had already stated that he and his gang were prepared for the journey. But the East, that is swift to wrath, is very slow over a bargain, and it is a point of doctrine besides, all the way from Gibraltar to Japan, to keep an American waiting if you hope to get the better of him. Ali Baba settled down for a nice long talk; and you would have thought, to judge by Grim's expression, that he could ask for nothing better.

The old rogue wanted to know among other things who would have the task of cleaning rifles on the journey. It seemed that he was long on sanctity, and not allowed by his religion to touch grease in any shape or form. Grim satisfied him on that point. Narayan Singh should clean the rifles.

But that started him off on a new trail. He tried to see how much more he could impose on the Sikh, and suggested such matters as pitching tents, cooking, gathering firewood, cleaning pots and pans, leading the pack-camels, and a host of other necessary evils.

"I shall issue all needful orders to each man," Grim told him bluntly at last.

"And what is to be done to Ali Higg?"

"That remains to be seen."

"He is a devil with a cold face."

"So I'm told."

"He has more than a hundred armed men."

"I heard twice that number."

"And we shall be twenty?"

"Twenty."

"Oh, well, Allah makes all things easy!"

But that was not the last word. There was still a custom of the country to be met and overcome.

"Are the camels watered?" Grim asked.

"Surely."

"Packs all ready?"

"All tied up-everything."

"You're all ready to start, then?"

"Inshallah bukra."[4]

"Tomorrow won't help me," said Grim. "We start tonight, at sundown. I'll go with you and look the camels over now."

"But, Jimgrim, that is impossible. My son Mahommed's second wife is sick--"

"Leave him behind, then, to look after her."

"He will not consent to be left! Two of the camels are not paid for. The man comes in the morning for his money."

"Leave the money here for him with Captain de Crespigny. We start tonight."

"But what if the camels are not satisfactory?"

"I shall see about other ones at once in that case. There'll be time if we look them over now. We start tonight."

"I was thinking about some mules to carry an extra load or two."

"No. Don't want mules. Too hot for them. Besides, there's no time for changing the loads over. We start tonight."

"Tomorrow will be a better moon, Jimgrim."

"We want a full moon when we get to Petra. We start tonight. Come along;

---

4   Tomorrow, if God is willing.

show me the camels."

"It is hot now. There is a bad stink in the stables. Better see them when it gets cooler."

"I'm going now. Are you coming with me?"

"Taib. I will show them to you. They are good ones. They will make you proud. Better give them another night's rest, though, Jimgrim."

"Come along. Let's look at them."

"One has a little girth-gall that--"

"Ali Baba, you old rogue, we start tonight!" said Grim.

CHAPTER II

"Trust in God, But Tie Your Camel!"

Do you believe in portents? I do. Whenever in the East the first two statements that a man has made in my presence, and that I have a chance to test, prove accurate, I go ahead and bet on all the rest. I don't mean by that that because a man has told the truth twice he won't lie on the third and fourth occasion; for the East is like the West in that respect, and usually seeks to turn its virtue into capital. But in a land where, as old King Solomon, who knew his crowd, remarked, "All men are liars," you must have some sort of weathervane by which to guide your national optimism, so I settled on that one long ago.

Ali Baba had said there was a bad stink in the camel stables. A natural expert in hyperbole, he had not exaggerated in the least. And he had said that they were good camels; it was true. You did not need to be a camel expert to know those great long-legged Syrian beasts for winners. They looked like the first pick of a whole country-side, as he maintained they were--twenty-five of them in one string, representing an investment at after-war prices of the equivalent of five or six thousand U.S. dollars.

"Who has been looted to pay for these?" asked Grim.

"Allah! You have put an end to our proper business, Jimgrim. What could we do? We took our money and bought these camels, thinking to take a hand in the caravan trade."

Grim looked into the old rogue's eyes and laughed.

"In the land I come from," he said, "a capitalist with your predatory instincts would pay a lawyer by the year to tell him just how far he could safely go!"

"A *wakil?*" sneered Ali Baba. "The *wakils* are all scoundrels. May Allah grind their bones! No honest man can have the advantage of such people."

Grim looked the loads over, but there was nothing that any one could teach that gang about desert work. The goat-skin water-bags were newly patched and moist; the gear was all in good shape, none new, but all well-tested; and there was food enough in double sacks for twenty men for a month. Mujrim, Ali Baba's giant oldest son, picked up the loads and turned them over for Grim to examine with about as much apparent effort as if he were tossing pillows.

Presently Grim laughed again, and looked at the line of fifteen other sons and grandsons, all squatting in the shadow of the wall watching us.

"Which is the chief Lothario?" he asked; only he used a much more expressive word than that, because the East is frank where the West deals in innuendo, and vice versa.

"They are all grown men," said Ali Baba. "There's a woman named Ayisha--a Badawi (Bedouin)--who has lately come from El-Maan with a caravan of wheat merchants."

"How did you know that, Jimgrim?"

"I'm told she has been buying things in the *suk*[5] that no Badawi could have use for, and has sent to Jerusalem for goods that could not be obtained here. I want to speak with her. Has any of your"--he smiled at the line of placidly contented sons again--"fathers of immorality made her acquaintance by some chance?"

Every one of the sixteen sons instantly assumed an expression of far-away meditation. Ali Baba looked shocked.

"I see!" said Grim. "Um-m-m! Well--none of my business. But one of you go fetch her to the governorate. You may tell her she's not in trouble, but an officer wants first-hand information about El-Maan."

"Shall my sons be seen dragging a woman through the streets?" asked Ali Baba.

"Let's hope not. But I don't care to send the police. I don't want to put her to indignity, you understand. Suppose you arrange it for me, eh?"

"Listen, Jimgrim; that woman is a strange one! Men have spoken evil of her, but none can prove it. I have heard it said she has a devil. `Trust in God, but tie your camel!' says the Book.[6] The wisest among wise men would be he who let that

5 Bazaar
6 The Moslems attribute all their favorite proverbs to the Koran, whether they are in the book or,

woman alone!"

"I suppose I'll have to get Captain de Crespigny to arrange it for me."

"Tfu![7] There is no need for a man like you to appeal to the governor. *Taib.* It shall be done. Have no doubt of it."

"All right. Send her up to the governorate--and no delays, mind! We start to-night at sundown."

On our way back we met Narayan Singh returning from the *suk* with parcels under his arm. That in itself was a sure sign of the lapse of contact with law and order; in Jerusalem he would have had an Arab carry them, because dignity is part of a Sikh's uniform. You realized without a word said that the uniform would be discarded presently. He looked me up and down as the quartermaster eyes a new recruit, and nodded in that exasperating way that makes you feel as if you had been ticketed and numbered. If Grim had not told me that the Sikh had been first to suggest taking me to Petra I would have insulted him painstakingly there and then; but you learn a certain amount of self-restraint, I suppose, before such a man as Narayan Singh ever approves of you for any purpose.

He undid the parcels on the dining-room table in the governorate, and the next half-hour was spent in rigging me up as an ascetic-looking Indian Moslem, with the aid of a white turban wound over a cone-shaped cap, great horn-rimmed spectacles, and the comfortable, baggy garments that the un-modernized *hakim* wears over narrow cotton pantaloons.

Over it all they put a loose, brown Bedouin cloak of camel-hair such as any man expecting to travel across deserts might invest in, whatever his nationality; it was hotter than Tophet, but, as the Arabs say, what keeps the heat in will also keep it out. It gives you a feeling of carrying your home around with you on your back, the way a snail totes its shell, and there are worse sensations.

"Now consider yourself a while in the mirror, sahib," said Narayan Singh. "When a man knows how he looks he begins to act accordingly."

Have you ever stopped to think how true that is? There was a full-length mirror upstairs in de Crespigny's bedroom, left behind by a German missionary's wife when the Turks and their friends stampeded, and Narayan Singh watched while I

---

as in this case, not.

7   An exclamation of contempt

posed in front of it. Before many minutes, without any deliberately conscious effort on my part, gesture and attitude were molding themselves to fit the costume, in somewhat the same way, I suppose, that a farm-hand from Montenegro shapes himself into a new American store suit.

"But it is necessary to remember!" warned Narayan Singh. "We should have done this sooner. There should be a photograph to carry with you, because a man forgets his own appearance where there are no mirrors and none others resembling himself. Henceforward, sahib, sleeping or waking, be a *hakim!* There is a chest of medicines downstairs."

By the time I had got down Grim had already changed into Bedouin dress--stepped simply out of one world into another. All he does is to stain his eyebrows dark, put on the clothes, and cease to resemble anything on earth except a desert-born Arab. I don't know how long he was learning to make the transformation, but no man could learn the trick in twenty years unless he loved the desert and the sinewy men who live in it.

He looked me over again narrowly, and then decided I must return upstairs and shave my head. "The only chance you've got of not being pulled apart between four camels, or pushed over a precipice, is to look like darwaish. Have Narayan Singh stain the back of your neck with henna--not too much of it--just a little--you're from Lahore, you know--a university product."

By the time I had carried out that order I could not even recognize myself without the turban on. "No matter how many mistakes now, Sahib!" grinned the Sikh. "None but a crazy Moslem would travel in this sun with his head shaved. Better put a cloth inside the cap, thus, for greater safety."

The only other thing Grim did to me was to throw away my toothbrush.

"They're suspicious in these parts," he said. "They'd figure it was hog-bristles. You'll have to make shift with a chewed stick, and pick your teeth between times with a dagger the way the rest of us do. Hello! Here she comes. You do the honors, 'Crep; we're in the game from now on."

De Crespigny went to the door and Grim and I squatted cross-legged in the window-seat. I tried to feel like a middle-aged native of the East under the rule of that twenty-six-year-old governor; but it couldn't be done. I don't know yet what the sensations are of, say, a bachelor of arts of Lahore University who has to take orders from a British subaltern. I expect you have to leave off pretending and really be an Indian to find out that; otherwise your liking for the fellow himself offsets reason. No white man could have helped liking young de Crespigny.

He came in after a minute perfectly self-possessed, leading a young woman who took your breath away. I have heard all the usual stories about the desert women being hags, but every one of them was pure fiction to me from that minute. If all the rest were really what men said of them, this one was sufficiently amazing to redeem the lot. De Crespigny addressed her as Princess, and she may have really ranked as one for all I know.

She sat on a chair, rather awkwardly, as if not used to it, and we stared at her like a row of owls, she studying us in return, quite unabashed. The Badawi don't wear veils, and are not in the least ashamed to air their curiosity. She stared uncommonly hard at Grim.

Of middle height, supple and slender, with the grace of all outdoors, smiling with a dignity that did not challenge and yet seemed to arm her against impertinence, not very dark, except for her long eyelashes--I have seen Italians and Greeks much darker--she somewhat resembled the American Indian, only that her face was more mobile.

Part of her beauty was sheer art, contrived by the cunning arrangement of the shawl on her head, and kohl on her eyelashes. That young woman knew every trick of deportment down to the outward thrust of a shapely bare foot in an upturned Turkish slipper. Her clothing was linen, not black cotton that Bedouin women usually wear, and much of it was marvelously hand-embroidered; but all the jewelry she wore was a necklace made of gold coins. It gave a finishing touch of opulence that is the crown of finished art.

But it was her eyes that took your breath away, and she was perfectly aware of it; she used them as the desert does all its weapons, frankly and without reluctance, sparing no consideration for the weak--rather looking for weakness to take advantage of it. They were wise--dark, deadly wise--alight with youth, and yet amazingly acquainted with all evil that is older than the world. She was obviously not in the least afraid of us.

"You are from El-Maan?" asked de Crespigny, and she nodded.

"Did you come all this way alone?"

"No woman travels the desert alone."

"Tell me how you got here."

"You know how I got here. I came with a caravan that carried wheat--the wife of the sheikh of the caravan consenting."

She spoke the clean concrete Arabic of the desert, that has a distinct word for everything, and for every phase of everything --another speech altogether from the jargon of the towns.

"Are they friends of yours?"

"Who travels with enemies?"

"Did you know them, I mean, before you came with them?"

"No."

"Then you are not from El-Maan?"

"Who said I was?"

"I thought you did."

"Nay, the words were yours, khawaja."[8]

"Please tell me where you come from."

"From beyond El-Maan."

She made a gesture with one hand and her shoulder that suggested illimitable distances.

"From which place beyond El-Maan?"

She laughed, and you felt she did it not in self-defense, but out of sheer amusement.

"Ask the jackal where his hole is! My people live in tents."

"Well, Princess, tell me, at any rate, what you are doing here in El-Kalil."[9]

"Ask El-Kalil. The whole *suk* talks of me. I have made purchases."

"That's what I'm getting at. You've made some unusual purchases, and you've sent to Jerusalem for things that people don't use as a rule in tents out in the desert-- silk stockings, for instance, and a phonograph with special records, and soft pillows, and writing-paper, and odds and ends like that. Do you use those things?"

"Why not?"

"Do you use books in French and English?"

She hesitated. It was the first time she had not seemed perfectly at ease.

8   Lit., gentleman-sir
9   Hebron

"Can you even read Arabic?"

She did not answer.

"Then the books, at any rate, are meant for some one else? Tell me who that some one is."

"Allah!" she exploded "May I not buy what I will, if I pay for it?"

But that was a false move. You can't upset the young British officer by storming at him. De Crespigny smiled, and came back at her with his next question suddenly.

"Are not those things for the wife of Ali Higg, and are you not from Petra?"

"If you know so surely whence I come, why do you ask me?"

"Are you a slave?"

"Allah!"

"How many wives has Ali Higg?"

"How should I know?"

"Because I think you are one of his wives. Is that not so?"

"I am Ayisha. I claim Your Honor's protection."

That was no false move. It was so nearly a checkmate that de Crespigny went to the sideboard for the silver box of cigarettes, to offer her one and gain time for thought.

Ever since the days of Ruth, and no doubt long before that, it has been the first law of the desert that man or woman claiming protection can no longer be treated as an enemy. It is possibly the earliest form of freemasonry, and it survives.

Arab history is full of instances of a warrior laying down his life for an enemy who has claimed protection from him. And young de Crespigny was ruler of the most unruly city in the Near East because he understood better than most men how to respect Arab prejudices. Ayisha accepted a cigarette, fitted it into a long amber tube, and watched him.

"Very well," he said at last. "If I protect you you must answer questions. Are you Ali Higg's wife?"

"Have I Your Honor's promise of protection?"

"Yes. Are you Ali Higg's wife?"

"I am his second wife."

"Thought so! And you've been sent to make purchases for number one?"

She nodded.

"How do you propose to convey all these things back to Petra?"

"Surely it is not difficult now that I am promised Your Honor's protection!"

"My district extends half-way to Beersheba and to the eastward as far as the shore of the Dead Sea--no farther," said de Crespigny.

"I can wait. I must wait for the purchases from Jerusalem. Sooner or later there will be a caravan across the desert to El-Maan. I have two servants here to make inquiries for me."

"Yes, and two more who went to Jerusalem. Four men. Tell me this, Princess Ayisha: how came Ali Higg to trust you, alone with four men, on such a long and difficult journey?"

"Is he not my lord?"

"But the men?"

"Is he not also their lord? And he holds their wives and sons in trust at Petra."

"You'll admit it's unusual?"

"Do you find it strange that a woman should be faithful to her lord?"

"But to Ali Higg? He has a name--a reputation! How many wives has he?"

"The Koran permits but four. The others are not wives."

"And you're going back?"

"Inshallah."[10]

It was obvious that no alternative would have the least appeal for her.

"Well, your movements have all been known to me. Your men have been watched. The word from Jerusalem is that the two you sent there have made their purchases. I heard over the telephone that they are on their way here. A suggestion has been made to me that you five might be held here as hostages to bring Ali Higg to terms."

She laughed. "He would raid, and make prisoners, ten for one. If an exchange were not made promptly his prisoners would be put to torture, and--"

De Crespigny saw fit to bring the conversation back to its other foot, as it were. Not the whole British Army was in a position just then to impose its will on Ali Higg, so certainly de Crespigny was not; and if you are any kind of real diplomatist, with a career in front of you, you don't talk fight unless you mean it.

---

10 If God is willing

"But of course, as you've claimed my protection I couldn't dream of that," he assured her. "Now, is there anything else you want after those men get here from Jerusalem?"

"Nothing else."

"They'll be here in an hour or so. Would you be ready to leave at once for Petra?"

"As soon as I can join a caravan."

"Today? This evening, for instance?"

"Allah provide it!"

"That's settled, then."

He turned toward Grim.

"This is Sheik Hajji,[11] Jimgrim bin Yazid of El-Abdeh, who has twice made the pilgrimage to Mecca. He is my honored friend. He starts tonight with a caravan toward Petra. You may travel with him and be in safe hands all the way."

She eyed Grim curiously, startled, it seemed to me. Then her expression changed slowly to excitement, followed by a look of baffling wisdom, as much as to say she knew something and would not tell. I don't think it was his name that startled her; that sounded Arabic enough.

"What business has he at Petra?" she asked.

De Crespigny let Grim answer that conundrum.

"Ya sit Ayisha,"[12] said Grim, "I carry a letter to Sheikh Ali Higg from some one in Arabia. I will deliver you along with the letter. You may have a place in my caravan--provided you have camels, provisions, and a litter," he added; for the surest way to increase her already alert suspicion would have been to offer to provide everything.

"Let me see the letter!"

Grim produced one instantly--an envelop with a big red seal on it. It was marked across the top in large letters "On His Majesty's Service," but addressed in Arabic to somebody, and as she could not read she was satisfied.

"Ali Higg will hold you answerable for my safety if he has to destroy armies to reach you!" she said simply.

11   One who has made the pilgrimage to Mecca
12   O lady Ayisha.

"Ya sit Ayisha," Grim answered solemnly, "may Allah turn my face cold if Sheikh Ali Higg shall have fault to find with me in this matter!"

"How many is in your caravan?" she asked. "Twenty armed men."

She nodded. "I will pay for my place in the caravan, according to the custom--the half now and the other half on arrival."

Without gesture, without moving a muscle of his face, Grim turned down that proposal desert-fashion, that is emphatically, with a reservation.

"Ya sit Ayisha, may Allah do so to me, and more, if I will accept a price for this. Between Ali Higg and me let this thing be."

"Taib," she answered. "My men shall look for camels. I will go with you to-night."

She went away then, leaving a smile behind her that would have coaxed the Sphinx, and rode down-street toward the ancient city on a big gray donkey guarded by two Bedouins armed with swords and spears.

"Did I do all right?" asked de Crespigny.

"Fine!" Grim answered. "You'll be ruling England one of these days, 'Crep. Good job I had that letter to show her, though, wasn't it?"

CHAPTER III

"Ali Higg's Brains Live in a Black Tent!"

I hate to have to admit that there was any virtue in Suliman, or anything other than vice in his new chum Abdullah. The two little devils stole my cigarettes, and deviled me unmercifully about my disguise, making improper jokes, at which Ali Baba and his sons laughed uproariously, and which they recalled at intervals for days afterwards.

But almost immediately after the "lady Ayisha" had left the governorate I was forced to admit that the brats were useful. In their own way they served Grim as a pair of hounds work for a man out hunting rabbits, for they could penetrate places and be welcome where a grown man would be killed--at the very least--for intruding or attempting to intrude. Harems, for instance. And they could be naive and wheedling toward a woman when they chose.

They came in with their tongues hanging out like a pair of pups, and sticky with the awful stuff men sell for candy in the El-Kalil bazaars. Evidently some woman had been pumping them for information, and Grim made them stand in front of him on the carpet.

"Well?"

They both spoke at once. Now and then one paused for breath and then the other, but on the whole it was a neck-and-neck race to tell the tale first.

"There was a woman in the *suk* who had heard of Jimgrim but never saw him, and she bought us sweets and took us to her house, and she asked us questions about Jimgrim, and we told lies, and she asked us what we were doing in El-Kalil, and we said nothing, and she said *wallah!* That was very little, and then she asked us all over again about Jimgrim. (*Gasp*)

"So we said Jimgrim has already gone back to Jerusalem, and she did not believe; but we swore by the beard of the Prophet, so she said what were we going to do now, and we said we would go to the governorate and beg for bread. (*Gasp*)

"So she said what next, and we said there is a great sheikh here from Arabia, who makes a journey to Petra, and *inshallah* he will take us with him, and she said why did we want to go to Petra, and we said because our mothers were carried off by the Turks and sold to the Arabs and *inshallah* we should find them near Petra. (*Gasp*)"

"So far, good!" said Grim. "That's what she got out of you. Now what did you get out of her?"

"She said *wallah!* There is Ali Higg at Petra and he grinds the face of the poor and is a great chief and will make us prisoners and sell us for slaves or have us turned into eunuchs, and we said (*gasp*) that we are *msakin*[13] and not afraid of Ali Higg and he may as well have us as anybody, and if it is written that we shall be eunuchs then it is written and who shall change it? (*Gasp*)

"And she said what made us think that the great sheikh will take us to Petra, and we said because he had promised, but he may be a big liar and we don't know yet."

"What kind of woman is she?" Grim asked.

"A big fat woman with a belly like two waterbags one on top of the other, thus!"

"What is her name?"

"She is the wife of Ismail ben Rafiki, the wool-dealer."

"Uh-huh. Yes. Go on."

"So she said we should come back here and find out if the sheikh will really take us and say to the sheikh (*gasp*) there is a lady in the city who can be of service to him in a certain matter and he should come back with us and we should lead him to the house and she will give us money and the sheikh will understand."

"Good!" pronounced Grim. "Not half bad. Just for that I'll go with you."

He winked at de Crespigny, nodded to me, pulled on a black-and-white striped Bedouin cloak, and went off with them at once. Whereat Narayan Singh came in, looking like another person altogether, although, if anything, bigger than before.

13 Poverty-stricken

He had got out of uniform and was dressed in a medley of Indian and Arab costume that made him look like one of those slaves in the "Arabian Nights" who cut off the heads of women. All he needed was a big curved simitar to fill the bill.

"Henceforth I am the *hakim's* servant," he said, showing his teeth in an enormous grin. "Only," he added, "since it will be I who instruct the *hakim,* in secret the sahib must listen to me."

He got out the medicine-chest, and being a Sikh with all of a soldier's opinion of civilians proposed to teach me what the labels on the little bottles stood for. Even he laughed after a minute or two, when he had got himself thoroughly sewed up and called each bottle by its wrong name.

"Ah! What does it matter!" he exclaimed at last. "Sore eyes--broken leg--boils--knife-wound--let it be all one. Give episin salts--always episin. Then, if we are long in one place, so that a sick man comes a second time, swearing grievously because of episin, give croton. That person will not come again, but the fame of the *hakim* will spread far and wide."

"You'd much better teach me how a *hakim* sits a camel," I suggested.

"All ways, sahib, for the *hakim* is not seldom a *bunnia* whose parents bought him education. Softer than wax is the rump of a *bunnia* and one who reads books. He sits this way until the boils break out, and then that way until the skin chafes. Then presently he lies across the saddle on his belly and either prays or curses, according as his spirit is pious or otherwise. But the camel continues to proceed, since that is its nature."

"Well, go on, instruct the *hakim,* then. The sahib listens."

"It is well to remember there will be with us, besides those seventeen thieves of this place, who know who we truly are, four sons of the desert and a woman. Now the woman, being woman, and they are all alike, will take note of the *hakim* and pretend to little sickness for the sake of making talk. Whereas the men, being, as it were, the guardians of the woman, will be seized with pride and jealousy. So that what with the woman's curiosity and the men's watchfulness there will be great need for discretion."

"How would you define discretion?"

"In the case of the woman, insolence. In the case of the men, a good humor--with perhaps some such physic for quarrelsomeness as croton oil administered in their food on suitable occasion. Whenever they get suspicious, sahib, drench their food!

"When the woman makes great eyes and shams complaints, tell her what their cursed Prophet said of women. Never mind whether he said it or not, sahib, for she will not know the truth of it, never having read the book. Only speak evil of all women, and so we shall come to Ali Higg's nest in good repute."

"All right. I'll try not to flirt with the lady. What next?"

"The sahib will be accused of being a Persian, and will be insulted accordingly, for none loves a Persian in this land, Islam having two chief sects, of which the Persians chose to adopt the Shia faith, which is not in favor with the Sunni, who are most numerous and most fanatic. The less the Sunni knows of his religion the more he despises a Shia; and when these people despise they steal, strike, abuse, and act otherwise unseemly."

"But I'm not supposed to be a Persian, am I?"

"No, for you could never act a Persian's part. But they will accuse you of being a Persian because you are an Indian, as I have heard a man called a dago because he was born somewhere south of a certain line. When it has been established that you are no Persian, but an Indian, it must be remembered that there are only two kinds of Indians whom they do not despise, and they are Sikhs and Pathans--Sikhs, because a Sikh can smite three Arabs with one hand, and the Pathan for much the same reason.

"But I must not go as a Sikh because of the religious difficulty; neither may you be a Pathan, because you in no way resemble one, nor do you speak the Pushtu tongue. But I will be a Pathan, because I can speak that language; therefore they will respect me as a man prone to fight readily and well. And knowing that no Pathan would demean himself by being servant to a man of no account, they will more readily respect you, although you are neither Sikh nor yet Pathan but are supposed to be a Punjabi Mussulman. Therefore, sahib, you must take a middle course between peace and pugnacity, pretending on the one hand to restrain my quarrelsomeness, yet on the other depending for safety on my readiness to take offense--as a man who is accustomed to a servant of mettle."

The rest of his lecture was about niceties of behavior, religious observances, and so on. It was a mystery how that man had never been promoted. He seemed to have eyes for everything and a memory for everything that he had ever observed. The Sikh despises the religion of Islam quite as fervently as the follower of the Prophet scorns Sikhism; yet he seemed familiar with every detail of Moslem custom, and knew to what extent geography affected it. The point he seemed to understand best was how to turn the flank of ignorant fanaticism.

"Whenever you make a mistake, sahib, remember this: you are Darwaish, which is a man who is privileged, having set behind him all unimportant matters. So when you are accused of not observing this or that, or of acting with impropriety, confound the Bedouin always by sneering at their ignorance, saying that where you come from men know what is proper. And Jimgrim, having truly made the pilgrimage to Mecca, will confound them likewise, having knowledge, whereas most of these rascals only know by hearsay."

I suppose he lectured me for two hours, until Grim came in looking pleased with himself, followed by the two infants looking much more pleased. You can't mistake the adventurous air of an eight-year-old with money hidden on his person, whatever his nationality may be. De Crespigny followed them in to learn the news.

"Know anything about old Rafiki, the wool-merchant?" Grim asked.

"Steady-going old party," said de Crespigny. "Says his prayers, cheats his customers, keeps the curfew law, and runs a three-wife establishment, I believe, in three parts of town, all according to the Book. Why, have you run foul of him?"

"He has offered me ten thousand piastres to poison Ali Higg"

"Show me the money!" laughed de Crespigny.

"He was hardly as previous as that. His head wife bribed these kids to bring me to the house, and the old boy met me in the wool-store. Said he'd been told I was going to Petra.

"First suggestion he made was that I should take my time on the road and way-lay a caravan that's sure to follow. He'd no idea, of course, that the lady Ayisha is to travel with me. His little scheme is to provide her with camels and men on his own account--mean camels and his own men, who would run away at the first sign of trouble.

"He assumes that I'm a gay Lochinvar who'd like nothing better than to carry off the lady. He wants her carried off and ravished as a spite for Ali Higg."

"Well, I didn't exactly fall for that; said I couldn't very well approach Ali Higg afterward, and he admitted that relations in that case might be kind o' strained. So he proposed next that I should meet up with Ali Higg and poison him. He offered to supply the poison--stuff that he said would make him die slowly in agony."

"What's his quarrel with Ali Higg?"

"Seems the old boy had a daughter who was the apple of his eye--or so he said. She was on her way down to Egypt; and I suspect she did not travel by train because she's been bought by some beast of a pasha. They didn't want inquiries by passport people, or any interfering bunk like that.

"Anyhow, Ali Higg is quite a ladies' man, and he happened to be crossing the map with part of his gang of thieves somewhere down Beersheba way. He agreed with the pasha on the point of taste and carried off the girl. So old wool-merchant Rafiki had to refund the purchase-price--not that he admitted that to me, of course.

"I suspect that's where the rub comes. If he hadn't been selling the girl illegally he'd surely have complained to you about the rape in the first instance. As it was he couldn't think of anything except revenge.

"I asked him if he'd take the girl back, and he said no, what should he do with her? What he wants is money, or else the lingering death of Ali Higg; and seeing it's about as easy to get money out of that gentleman as cream cheese out of the moon, he's willing to part with a hundred pounds for either of two things--the rape of Ayisha or the death of Ali Higg. On those terms he vows he'd die contented."

"If he finds out that Ayisha goes with you tonight he'll try to corrupt old Ali Baba or one of his sons," said de Crespigny.

"Yes, and he probably will find it out. But corrupting Ali Baba would take time and a lot of money; and none of his sons dares do a thing without the old man's approval. I feel fairly sure of the gang. Point is, do you know of any other gang that the wool-merchant could hire right now to attack us somewhere on the road?"

"There's none in Hebron that would dare. Plenty outside in the villages."

"The lady Ayisha has probably told that she's going tonight," said Grim. "Old Woolly-wits might not find it out until too late, but I suspect his wives get all the gossip that's going. Then he'll have to work fast, because we shall move fast. What villages does he trade with chiefly?"

"The Beni-Assan and the Beni-Khor."

"Small crowds, both of them. Counting her four fanatics, we'll be four-and-twenty armed men, and tough in the bargain. Is there any outlying sheikh who owes old Rafiki money? Who are his wives, for instance?"

"Now you're on the track," said de Crespigny. "One of his wives--the third, I think--is the daughter of Abbas Mahommed of the Beni-Yussuf tribe. Abbas Mahommed is always in debt to him."

"Where's his place?"

"Down near the lower end of the Dead Sea. Right near where you'll want to pitch your first camp. Abbas Mahommed sells him camel wool and hides, and goes in debt in advance regularly. This spring, for some reason, he delivered very little, and is still heavily in debt to Rafiki."

"How many men has he?"

"Might turn out fifty strong."

"That's where we're due for our first trouble, then," said Grim. "We'll have to put one over on him. I know one way of spoiling friend Rafiki's game; old Woolly-wits'll fall sure. Suppose you go and see him, 'Crep, or send for him, and ask him straight out to provide camels for the lady Ayisha. He'll send his own men along with them, of course, and give them private instructions. Let's see--four men and a woman plus provisions, and he'll probably send five men with them--twelve camels, eh? Who else can raise seven good camels in this place?"

"Easy. I know where to get 'em."

"Good. Hire them then. Tie them in two strings and send them out with two policemen to wait for us ten miles along the road. Be sure they start ahead of us. Soon as we overtake them I'll dismiss Rafiki's men, who'll be nothing but his spies, swap the princess and her four men and their loads on to the fresh beasts, and leave the police to chase Rafiki's experts home again. Will you do that?"

It was getting well along toward sunset, and de Crespigny had to hurry; but one of the advantages of being short-handed as administrator of a district is that you have to keep in intimate personal touch with all essentials, and there was not much that young de Crespigny did not know about getting what he wanted done in quick time. Within half an hour seven pretty good camels were sauntering southward out of Hebron, with a couple of phlegmatic Arab policemen perched on the two leaders, and the noses of the others tied to the empty saddles of the beasts ahead. They were neither as big nor in as good condition as old Ali Baba's wonderful string, but very likely better than any that the wool-merchant would provide, and by that much less likely to reduce our speed after we should make the change.

"You see how easy it is," said Grim, "for a rascal like Ali Higg to upset a whole country-side. Here we are getting the crime of Palestine running in grooves, as it were, so's to regulate it first and then reduce it to reasonable proportions, and all that beast needs do is steal a woman and start civil war."

But I did not see that the wool-merchant's private plans for vengeance amounted to civil war, and said so.

"Hah! Wait and see!" said Grim. "Woolly-wits goes after vengeance. Somebody gets killed. That means a blood-feud. All the relatives of the slain man--whether it's Ali Higg or one of his retainers doesn't matter--take up arms; and all the relatives of Woolly-wits do ditto. For each man killed in the war that follows the other side is out for the equivalent in life or goods. Village after village gets drawn in.

"Suppose that sheikh at the south end of the Dead Sea who's in debt to Woolly-wits jumps at the chance to loot our caravan and bag the lady, we'll be lucky if one or two of our men don't get scuppered. That means a blood-feud between that village and all old Ali Baba's clan.

"But that isn't nearly all, nor nearly the worst of it. Ali Higg learns next that the Dead Sea outfit have tried to waylay his wife; so he takes the warpath. And instead of that making a three-cornered fight of it, it might mean an offensive alliance between Ali Higg and Ali Baba's gang.

"Civil war would be a very mild name for that. There'd be brains brought to bear on it. The administration might have to spend twenty or thirty thousand pounds and jail a lot of estimable Arabs. The thing to do is to stop that kind of thing before it happens."

"By corraling Ali Higg, I suppose?" said I.

"Can't very well do that. He's a free man. Of course he's got no right to cross our border and steal women, but, on the other hand, he's made himself boss of a district that no other government pretends to control.

"If we can catch him our side of the line he's our meat; but that's reciprocal; if he can catch us on his side there's no law to prevent his doing what he likes with us. We've got to use our heads with Master Ali Higg."

I think that was the first time it really dawned on me that this venture was going to be dangerous. Even so, the calmness with which Grim considered leaving law and all the means of its enforcement behind and crossing deserts with a gang of known thieves for accomplices took most of the edge off it.

You simply couldn't feel scared when that fellow smiled and exposed the risks in detail, even with dark coming on and the sound of camels being made to kneel outside the window. For Ali Baba had become convinced at last that Grim really intended to start that night, and, making a virtue of necessity, was better than punctual. The camels were groaning and swearing, as they always do at the prospect of a night's work.

"As I see it, any tribe out there has as much right to elect Ali Higg leader as you and I have to elect a president," said Grim. "I don't suppose they did elect him, but they'll claim they did. The point is, he's got himself elected somehow. We've no veto. I don't hold with murder; it sets a bad example and turns loose a horde of individual trouble-makers who were under something like control before. It might be easy to have him murdered; you see how easy old Woolly-wits thought it might be. Murder has always been the solution of politics in the Old World right down to date; and look where they're at in consequence!"

"You must have some idea to go on," I suggested.

"What's your plan?"

"They say I look a bit like Ali Higg."

"But what then? Haven't you a plan--nothing you mean to try first?"

"Oh yes. *Chercher la femme.*"

"So there's a woman in it?"

"You bet! Ali Higg's no born statesman. His brains live in a black tent, and he keeps 'em encouraged with French and English books bought in Jerusalem--silk stockings--gramophones--all kinds of things."

"What is she--a Turk? I've heard some of them are educated nowadays."

"No. And she never was a Turk. She was born in Bulgaria of Greco-Russo-Bulgar parents, educated at Roberts College and Columbia University, New York, married to a drummer in the shredded-codfish business, divorced--on what grounds I don't know--divorced him, though, I believe came out here as war worker-teacher in refugee camps in Egypt--made the acquaintance of Ali Higg when he was prisoner of war down there--he was fighting for the Turks at one time--and helped him to escape.

"I've never set eyes on her, but they say she's a rare good-looker and has more brains in her little finger than most men keep under their hats. I'm told she has designs on the throne of Mesopotamia."

"Mespot? I thought the League of Nations was going to let the Arabs choose their own king."

"Sure. And as soon as she sees that Ali Higg's pretensions don't amount to a row of shucks I wouldn't give ten piastres for that gentleman's lease of life! Borgia had nothing on her, they tell me."

"So we're out to play chess with a white woman. Why didn't you tell me this before?"

"What's your hurry?" asked Grim. "If you find out too much all at once you'll lose your bearings. I'll introduce you to the lady if we ever reach Petra right side up. Now let's eat, and get a move on. A full belly for a long march! Come."

CHAPTER IV

"Go and Ask the Kites, then, At Dat Rasi"

So far everything worked out strictly according to plan. We had hardly finished a hurried meal when the lady Ayisha and her men arrived on mean baggage camels provided by old Rafiki; and they were not in the least pleased with their mounts, for a baggage camel is as different from a beast trained to carry a rider as an up-to-date limousine is from a Chinese one-wheel barrow. Perched on top of the lady Ayisha's beast was a thing they call a *shibrayah*--a sort of tent with a top like an umbrella, resting on the loads slung to the camel's flanks. From inside that she was busy abusing everybody.

There was only one good camel with her outfit--a small, blooded looking Bishareen, a shade or two lighter in color than the rest, ridden by a wiry, mean rascal with a very black face. He seemed anxious not to assert himself, for he kept his mount well away in the shadows, and moved off when any one approached him.

It was growing pitch-dark. Grim counted noses and gave the order to be off. Two or three men mounted, and that brought all the kneeling camels to their feet. One of Ali Baba's sons caught the beast assigned to me, brought him round to the gate, and began *nakhing* him to make him kneel again. But I know one or two things about Arabs and their ways of assessing humanity. Knowledge is for use.

"Do you mistake me for a cripple?" I asked, and instead of continuing to *nakh* in the camel language he pulled the beast's head down.

The trick is simple enough. You put your foot on the hollow of the camel's neck and swing into the saddle as he raises his head again. Men used to the desert despise you if you have to make your mount kneel in order to get on his back, pretty much as horsemen of other lands despise the tender foot who can't rope and saddle his own pony. There's no excuse for that, of course; it stands to reason that lots of first-class men can't mount a camel standing, never having done it; but, according to desert lore, whoever has to make his camel kneel is a person of no account.

So I started off with at least one minus mark not notched against me. There was also an enormous feeling of relief, because I heard those two brats blubbering at being left behind.

And oh, what a start that was before the moon-rise, with the great soft-footed beasts like shadows stringing one behind another into line through the streets of a city as old as Abraham! Utter silence, except for three camel bells with different notes. Instant, utter severance from all the new world, with its wheels that get you nowhere and conventions that have no meaning except organized whimsy.

Peace under the stars, wholly aloof and apart from the problem that had sent us forth. And the feel under you of league-welcoming resilience, whatever the camels might say by way of objection. And they said a very great deal gutturally, as camels always do, yielding their prodigious power to our use with an incomprehensible mixture of grouchiness and inability to do less than their best.

Grim rode in advance. His was the first camel bell that jangled with a mellow note somewhere in the darkness around the turn of a narrow street, or in a tunnel, where house joined house overhead. The lady Ayisha's was the second bell, three beasts ahead of me; she being the guest of honor as it were, or, rather, the prize passenger, it was important to know her whereabouts at any given moment. And last of all came old Ali Baba with the third bell announcing that all were present and correct. He and his men sat their camels with a stately pride more than half due to the rifles and bandoliers that had been served out.

That black-faced fellow on the little Bishareen did not trouble himself about position in the line as long as we wound through the city streets. He was next in front of me, and I saw him exchange signals with a fat man in a house door, who may have been Rafiki the wool-merchant. Narayan Singh was next behind me, and I looked back to make sure that he had seen the signal too.

But when we passed out of the city at the south end and began to swing along a white road at a clip that was plenty fast enough for the baggage beasts, the man in front of me urged his beast forward, thrusting others out of the way and getting thoroughly well cursed for it, until he rode next behind Grim.

Seeing that, Narayan Singh rode after him, flogging furiously, and got well cursed too. But nothing else in particular happened for several miles until we began to descend between huge hills of limestone and, just as the moon rose, came on the reserve camels waiting for us in the charge of two policemen in a hollow.

Then there began to be happenings. First there was shrill delight from Ayisha and a chorus of approval from her four men at the prospect of changing to reasonably decent mounts. Then a tumult of indignation from the wool-merchant's crowd--blunt refusal by them to consent to any change at all--threats--abuse--arguments--the roaring of camels who object on principle to everything, whatever it is, even to a chance to rest, because it hurts their backs to stand still loaded and over it all presently Grim's voice issuing orders in a tone he had when things go wrong.

Strange that they don't choose leaders more often for their voices! It's the most obvious thing in the world that a man with a silver tongue, as they call it, can swing and sway any crowd. If that man knows his own mind and has a plan worth spending effort on he can trumpet cohesion out of tumult and win against men with twenty times his brains. I don't doubt Peter the Hermit had a voice like a bellbuoy in a tide-rip. Grim pitched his above the babel so that every word fell sharp, clear, and manly. They began to obey him there and then.

But he could not attend to everything at once, and while he oversaw the changing of pack-saddles, and gave orders to the policemen to ride back on the camels behind Rafiki's men and see them safely into the city, that black-faced fellow on the Bishareen edged away, and in a moment was off at full gallop headed southwards. Narayan Singh was the first to see him go, but it was half a minute before he could get near Grim and call his attention to it.

Grim ordered three of Ali Baba's men in pursuit at once.

"Shall we shoot? Shall we slay?" asked one of them.

"No, no. He hasn't committed any crime yet. Catch him and bring him back."

"Crime? What is crime out here? We can kill him. But overtake him on that beast? *Wallah!*"

They wasted another minute arguing for leave to shoot, and by the time they were off the deserter had a long start; but they rode with a will when they did go.

If anything on earth looks more absurd than a ridden camel galloping away in the moonlight, with his neck stretched out in front of him and his four ungainly legs in the air all together, it is three more camels doing the same thing. They looked like a giant's washing blown off the line flapping before a high wind, and made hardly more noise. The whack-whack-whack of sticks on the beasts' rumps was as distinct as pistol-shots, but you hardly heard the galloping footfall.

Grim went on about his business, for changing loads in the dark is a job that needs attention, unless you choose to have a good beast lose heart before morning and lie down in the middle of the road. A camel in pain from a badly cinched girth will endure it without argument for just so long; after which he quits, and not all the whacking or persuading in the world will get him up again.

At the end of twenty minutes we were under way once more. Peace closed down on us, and we swayed along under the stars in majestic silence. There have been better nights since, I think; but until then that was the most glorious experience of a lifetime.

It is my peculiar delight to read and relive ancient history, and of all history books the Old Testament is vastly the most absorbing--far and away the most accurate. There is a school of fools who set themselves up to scoff at its facts, but every new discovery only confirms the old record; and here were we sauntering through the night on camels over hills where the fathers of history fought for the first beginnings of each man's right to do his own thinking in his own way.

After a while Ali Baba gave his camel bell to his oldest son Mujrim, and forced his beast up beside mine, seeming to think silence might ruin the nerve of such a raw hand as myself. Or perhaps it was pride of race and country that impelled him. Even the meanest Arab thrills with emotion when he contemplates his ancient heritage, just as he rages at the prospect of seeing the Jews return to it, and Ali Baba, though a prince of thieves, was surely not a man without a heart.

But the trouble with Arab as distinguished from Jewish history is that too little of it was written down, and too much of it invented to prove a theory--much like the stuff they put between the covers of school history books--so Ali Baba's lecture, although gorgeous fiction in its way, hardly enriched knowledge. Not that he was free from the latterday craving for accuracy whenever it might serve to bolster up the rest of the fabric.

"Yonder," he said, for instance, pointing toward the sky-line with a dramatic sweep of his arm, "they say that Adam and Eve are buried. But they lie!"

And having denounced that lie, he expected me to believe everything else he told me.

According to him every rock we passed had its history of jinn and spirits as well as battles, and he knew where the tomb was of every national saint and hero, every one of whom had apparently died within a radius of twenty miles. Some of them had died in two or three different places as far as I could make out from his account of them.

And what Abraham had not done on those hillsides in the way of miracles and war would not be worth writing in a book; whatever cannot be otherwise explained is set down to the Ancestor, the Arabs ranking Abraham next after Mohammed, because the patriarch built the Kaaba, or Mosque, at Mecca, that Mohammed centuries later on adopted for his new religion.

But even Ali Baba grew tired of acting historian at last, and once more silence settled down, broken only by the bells and the camels' gurgling, until about midnight we overhauled the three men who had been sent in chase of the fellow on the Bishareen. They had lost him, and were angry; for what should a man do except be angry in such a circumstance, unless he is willing to accept blame?

"You should have let us shoot, Jimgrim! Once I got close enough to have cut his beast's legs with my sword! You think this is like the city, where a policeman holds up a hand and men halt? Hah! Wallah! It was he who drew sword, and behold my camel's nose where he slashed at it! One finger's breadth closer and I would have had a sick beast on my hands--but he proved a blundering pig with his weapon and only made that scratch after all.

"However, it is your fault, Jimgrim! You have made us to be laughed at by that father of dunghills! His beast was the faster, and he got away, and vanished in the shadows."

So there we halted and held a conference, letting the camels kneel and rest for half an hour, while each man said his say in turn.

"That man is Rafiki's messenger," said Grim. "He is on his way to Abbas Mahommed, Sheikh of the Beni Yussuf, who owes Rafiki money. I think Rafiki is offering to forgo the debt if Abbas Mahommed will lie in wait for us and carry off this woman."

He did not ask for suggestions. There was no need. Every one of those cloaked and muffled rascals had a notion of his own on the spur of the moment, and was eager to get it adopted.

"Allah!" said Ali Baba. "Let us fight, then, with Abbas Mahommed, and plunder his harem instead! It is simple. We come on his village before dawn when those sons of Egyptian mothers[14] are asleep. We set fire to the thatch, and thereafter act as seems fit, slaying some and letting others escape!"

"Wallah! Let us ride straight through the village, set a light to it, and run," suggested Mujrim. "There isn't a woman in that place I would burden a camel with."

"Nevertheless, we should take some women to keep as hostages against the time when a blood-feud begins."

"And surely we shall carry off some camels."

"Aye! They have a horse or two as well. Abbas Mahommed trades with El-Kerak, and only last month acquired a fine brown mare that caught my eye."

"What are fifty men! We can fight twice fifty of such spawn as the Beni Yussuf."

"Wallah! They ran when the police paid them a visit. Ran from the police!"

"Yes, and were afraid to kill the Jew who sued Abbas Mahommed in the court for arrears of interest. They are cowards who dare not take their sheikh's part in a dispute."

"Better wait until dawn, and then ride by their village and defy them."

But the lady Ayisha had the most astonishing suggestion. She came out from under the curtains of the *shibrayah* and sat against her camel's rump to face the circle of armed men and instruct them.

"Taib!" she said scornfully. "Let this Abbas Mahommed come and take me. I have a knife for his belly in any event. You go on to Ali Higg and say his wife is in the hands of that scum. Ali Higg can cross the desert in three days, and by the evening of the fourth day there will be no village left, nor a man to call Abbas Mahommed by his name. If I haven't killed him already Abbas Mahommed will be carried off to Petra with the women, who shall watch what is done to him before they are apportioned with the other loot. That is simplest. Let Abbas Mahommed lift me if he dares!"

She was clearly a young woman not averse to experiences, as well as confident

---

14   To call any one an Egyptian is an Arab's notion of a perfect insult

of her lord's good will. But Grim had the peace of the border in mind; and the gang were not at all disposed to stand by meekly while Abbas Mahommed paid a debt so easily to a mere wool-merchant.

"I am an old man," said Ali Baba, "and must die soon. May He Who never sleeps[15] slay me before I see my sons afraid to fight Abbas Mahommed and all his host!"

"Let's talk like wise men and not fools," proposed Grim at last, and since he had let them have their say first they heard him in silence now. "The difficulty is that Abbas Mahommed's village lies at the corner of the Dead Sea. We must turn that corner. If we pass between him and the sea he has us between land and water. If we journey too far south to avoid him we lose at least a day and tire our camels out. A forced march now would mean that we must feed the camels corn, and we have none too much of it with us; whereas tomorrow the grazing will be passable, and farther on, where the grazing is poor, we shall need the corn."

"*Wallah!* The man knows."

"*Inshalla,* let there be a fight then!"

"Wait!" counseled Ali Baba. "I know this Jimgrim. There will be a deception and a ruse, but no fight. Listen to him. Wait and see!"

"I think we will travel to the southward," said Grim, "and halt at dawn out of sight of Abbas Mahommed's village. There let the camels graze. But I, and a few of us, will take the lady Ayisha's camel with the *shibriyah,* and draw near to the village. That black-faced rogue of Rafiki's will point us out to them, for he will recognize the *shibriyah.*

"Then when they come to seize the lady Ayisha they will find no woman in the litter. So they will believe that Rafiki's messenger has told lies that are blacker than his face, and will beat him and let us go."

"But if they do not let you go? They are ruffians, you know, Jimgrim."

"Then I shall find another way."

"And how will you account for being so few men, when Rafiki's messenger will have said we are at least a score?"

"Will that not be further proof that the man is a liar?"

"If I did not know you of old I would say that is a fool's plan," remarked Ali Baba,

---

15   A synonym for Allah

and his sons grunted agreement. "But you have a devil of resourcefulness. *Taib!* Let us try this plan and see what comes of it."

So we started off again to a running comment of contemptuous disapproval from the lady Ayisha, who seemed to think that no plan could be a good one unless it entailed murder. The farther we headed eastward, the nearer we came to the pale beyond which her lord and master's word was summary law, the more openly she advocated drastic remedies for everything, and the less she was inclined to take no for an answer.

However, her monologue was wasted on the moon, for no one argued with her. Grim led the way-off the highroad now, and down dark defiles that set the camels moaning, while their riders yelled alternately to Allah and apostrophized their beasts in the monosyllabic camel language. Camels hate downhill work, especially when loaded, and fall unless told not to in a speech they understand, in that respect strangely like children.

You had to look out in the dark, too, for the teeth of the camel behind, because they don't love the folk who drive them headlong into gorges full of ghosts, and one man's thigh or elbow makes as easy biting as the next.

Camels are no man's pets, and there is no explaining them. The fools will graze contentedly with shrapnel and high explosives bursting all about them, but go into a panic at the sight of a piece of paper in broad daylight. And when they think they see ghosts in the dark they act like the Gadarene swine, only making more noise about it.

I wouldn't have been the lady Ayisha going down some of those dark places for all the wealth of ancient Bagdad. Her *shibrayah* pitched and rolled like a small boat in a big sea, and whenever a rock leaned out over the narrow trail, or a scraggy old thorn branch swung, it was by a combination of luck and good carpentry that she was saved from being pitched down under the following camel's feet. Whoever made that *shibrayah* could have built the Ark.

But we came down through one last terrific gorge on to a level plain, where the camel-thorn grew in clumps and the heat radiating from the hills was like the breath from an oven door behind us. There the animals went best foot forward, as if they smelled the dawn and hoped to meet it sooner by hurrying. We had quite a job to keep back for the loaded beasts, and three or four men, instead of one, brought up the rear to prevent straggling.

Then, about an hour before dawn, in a hollow between sparsely vegetated sand-dunes, Grim ordered camp pitched, and in very few minutes there was a row of little cotton tents erected, with a small fire in front of each.

Most of the camels were turned out at once to graze off the unappetizing-looking thorns, sparse and dusty, that peppered the field of view like scabs on a yellow skin. There was no fear of their wandering too far, for if the camel ever was wild, as many maintain that he never was, that was so long ago that the whole species has forgotten it, and he wouldn't know what to do without his owner somewhere near.

He has to be used at night, because he will not eat at night; on the other hand, he refuses to sleep in the daytime; so there is a limit to what you can do with a camel, in spite of his endurance, and once in so many days he has to be given a twenty-four hour rest so that he may catch up on both food and sleep.

But on the dry plains such as where we were then they give less trouble than anywhere. For though they soon go sick on good corn, which a horse must have, they thrive and grow fat on desert gleanings; and whereas sweet water will make their bellies ache oftener than not, the brackish, dirty stuff from wells by the Dead Sea shore is nectar to them.

Have you ever seen twenty camels rolling all at once with their legs in the air, preparatory to making breakfast off dry thorns that you wouldn't dare handle with gloves on? If so, you'll understand that they're the perfect opposite of every other useful beast that lives.

But not all the camels were turned out. Grim chose Mujrim--Ali Baba's eldest son--a black-bearded, forty-year-old giant--two of the younger men, Narayan Singh and me; and with the lady Ayisha's beast in tow with the empty *shibrayah* set off directly the sun was a span high over the nearest dune.

We rode almost straight toward the sun, and in five minutes it appeared how close we were to the village whence danger might be expected. It was a straggling, thatched, squalid-looking cluster of huts, surrounded by a mud wall with high, arched gates. Only one minaret like a candle topped with an extinguisher pretended to anything like architecture, and even from where we were you could see the rubbish-heaps piled outside the wall to reek and fester. There was a vulture on top of the minaret, and kites and crows--those inevitable harbingers of man--were already busy with the day's work.

The village Arabs are perfunctory about prayer, unless unctuous strangers are in sight, who might criticize. So, although we approached at prayer-time, it was hardly a minute after we rose in view over a low dune before a good number of men were on the wall gazing in our direction. And before we had come within a mile of the place the west gate opened and a string of camel-men rode out.

The man at their head was the sheikh by the look of him, for we could see his striped silk head-dress even at that distance, and he seemed to have a modern rifle as against the spears and long-barreled muskets of the others. There were about two-score of them, and they rode like the wind in a half circle, with the obvious intention of surrounding us. Grim led straight on.

They rode around and around us once or twice before the man in the striped head-gear called a halt. He seemed disturbed by Grim's nonchalance, and asked our business with not more than half a challenge in his voice.

"Water," Grim answered. "Did Allah make no wells in these parts?"

It doesn't pay to do as much as even to suggest your real reason for visiting an Arab village, for they won't believe you in any case.

"What have you in the *shibriyah?*"

"Come and see."

The Sheikh Mahommed Abbas drew near alone, suspiciously, with his cocked rifle laid across his lap. His men began moving again, circling around us slowly--I suppose with the idea of annoying us; for that is an old trick, to irritate your intended victim until some ill-considered word or gesture gives excuse for an attack. But we all sat our camels stock-still, and, following Grim's example, kept our rifles slung behind us.

The sheikh was a rather fine-looking fellow, except for smallpox marks. He had a hard eye, and a nose like an eagle's beak; and that sort of face is always wonderfully offset by a pointed black beard such as he wore. But there was something about the way he sat his camel that suggested laziness, and his lips were not thin and resolute enough to my mind, to match that beard and nose. I would have bet on three of a kind against him sky-high, even if he had passed the draw.

He drew aside the curtain of the *shibrayah* gingerly, as if he expected a trick mechanism that might explode a bomb in his face.

"Mashallah! Where is the woman?" he exclaimed.

I found out then that I was right as to the way to play that supposititious poker hand. Grim had doped him out too, and answered promptly without changing a muscle of his face.

"Wallahi! Should I bring my wife to this place?"

"Allah! Thy wife?"

"Whose else?"

"It was Ali Higg's wife according to the tale!"

"Some fools swallow tales as the dogs eat the offal thrown to them! By the beard of God's Prophet, whom do you take me for?"

"Kif?[16] How should I know?"

"Go and ask the kites, then, at Dat Ras!"

"You are he? You are he who slew the-- *Shi ajib!*[17] Now I think of it they did say he was beardless. Nay! Are you--Speak! Who are you?"

"Does your wife wander abroad while you herd cattle?" Grim asked him.

"Allah forbid! But--"

"Is my honor likely less than yours?"

"Then you are Ali Higg?"

"Who else?"

"And these?"

"My servants."

"Your honor travels abroad with a scant escort!"

"Let us see, then, whether it is not enough! A tale was told me of a black-faced liar on a Bishareen dromedary who fled hither from El-Kalil last night to persuade the dogs of this place to bark in some hunt of his. There was mention made of a woman. My men pursued him along the road, but fear gave him wings. Hand him over!"

"Allah! He is my guest."

"Or let us see whether I cannot fire one shot and summon enough men to eat this place!"

---

16 What?
17 This is strange!

"That is loud talk. They tell me you travel with but twenty."

"Try me!"

You didn't have to be much of a thought-reader to know what was passing in that sheikh's mind. Supposing that Grim were really the notorious Ali Higg, he might easily have left Hebron with twenty men and have been joined by fifty or a hundred others in the night. Or there might be others on the way to meet him now. It was a big risk, for Ali Higg's vengeance was always the same; he simply turned a horde of men loose to work their will on the inhabitants of any village that defied him. The sheikh was not quite sure yet that he really sat face to face with the redoubtable robber, yet did not dare put that doubt to the test.

"Is that all Your Honor wants?" he asked. "Just that messenger?"

"Him and his camel--and another thing."

"What else, then? We are poor folk in this place. There has been a bad season. We have neither corn nor money."

"If I needed corn or money I would come and take them," Grim answered. "I have no present need. I give an order."

"Allah! What then?"

"It pleases me to camp yonder."

He made a lordly motion with his head toward the west.

"This side your village, then, all this day until sundown, none of your people venture."

"But our camels go to graze that way."

"Not this day. Today yours graze to the eastward."

"There is poor grazing to the eastward."

"Nevertheless, whoever ventures to the westward all this day does so in despite of me, and the village pays the price!"

"Allah!"

"Let Allah witness!" answered Grim.

And his face was an enigma; but half the puzzle was already solved because there was no suggestion of weakness there. It was the best piece of sheer bluffing on a weak hand that I had ever seen.

"Will Your Honor not visit my town and break bread with me?" asked Mahommed Abbas.

"If I visit that dung-hill it will be to burn it," Grim answered. "Send me out that black-faced liar and the Bishareen. I am not pleased to wait long in the sun."

"If we obey the command do we not merit Your Honor's favor?"

That was a very shrewd question. A weak man with a weak hand would have walked into that trap by betraying the spirit of compromise. On the other hand an ordinary bluffer would have blundered by overdoing the high hand.

"Consider what is known of me," Grim answered. "How many have disobeyed me and escaped? How many have obeyed and regretted it? But by the beard of Allah's Prophet," he thundered suddenly, "I grow weary of words! What son of sixty dogs dares keep me waiting in the desert while he barks?"

Mahommed Abbas did not like that medicine, especially in front of all his men. But they had ceased circling long ago and were waiting stock-still at a respectful distance; for the name of Ali Higg meant evidently more to them than the honor of their own sheikh--which at best depends on the sheikh's own generalship. It was a safe bet that if he had called on them to attack that minute they would have declined.

So he gave the dignified Arab salute, which Grim deigned to acknowledge with the slightest possible inclination of the head, and led his men away.

"What would you have done if he had called your bluff?" I asked Grim, as soon as they were all out of earshot.

"Dunno," he said, smiling. "I've learned never to try a bluff unless I'm pretty sure of my man. That guy doesn't own many chips. As a last resort I'd have to admit I'm a government officer--if they hadn't killed us all first!"

We sat our camels there for about three quarters of an hour before half a dozen of Mahommed Abbas' men appeared with Rafiki's messenger riding the Bishareen between them. His face when they handed him over was the color of raw liver, and if ever a man was too scared to try to escape it was he. Ali Baba's two sons got one on either side of him without making him feel any better, for he too was a Hebron man and knew them and their reputation. There was nothing improbable about their throwing in their lot with the greater robber Ali Higg.

Then the sheikh's men tried to load gifts on Grim--chickens, a live sheep, melons, vegetables, and camel milk in a gourd. Grim did not even deign to acknowledge them in person, but made a gesture to Narayan Singh, who promptly took charge of the prisoner himself and sent Ali Baba's sons back for the presents. They had the good grace to find fault with everything, vowing that the sheep especially was only fit for vultures. However, with a final sneer or two anent the donor's manners they bore sheep and all along behind us back to camp.

"Is it well?" called Ali Baba, watching on the ridge of a dune, and coming to life like a heron as soon as we drew near.

"All's well," said Grim.

"Father of cunning! What now?" the old man answered.

CHAPTER V

"Let that Mother of Snakes Beware"

The terms that Grim had imposed on Abbas Mahommed were perfectly well understood by every one concerned. The Arab is an individualist of fervid likes and dislikes and the thing that perhaps he hates most of all is to be observed by strangers; he does not like it even from his own people. So there was nothing incomprehensible, but quite the reverse, about that requirement that none from the village should trespass in our direction all that day. And, of course, only a bold robber conscious of his power to enforce them would have dared to insist on such terms. But it was a good thing that Mahommed Abbas did not call the bluff.

As it was, we slept all morning undisturbed, with only four watchers posted, relieved at intervals of one hour. And the only disturbance we suffered was from the lady Ayisha, who insisted that the black-faced prisoner was hers, camel and all, and that he should be taken to Petra for summary execution. She threatened Grim with all sorts of dire reprisals in case he should let the man go.

But setting every other consideration aside the man would have been dangerous company on the journey. He was putting two and two together in his own mind, and was not nearly as frightened as he had been. But in Hebron he could do no harm, for once the Dead Sea should be behind us it would not matter how many people knew of Grim's errand, since we should travel faster than rumor possibly could across the desert.

But if he should get one chance to talk with the lady Ayisha's men, and even cause them to suspect that Grim might be in league in some way with the British authorities, it would be all up with our prospect of deceiving folk in future. There was danger enough as it was that one of Ali Baba's men might make some chance remark that would inform Ayisha or her escort.

Grim decided finally to let the man escape and gave Narayan Singh and me instructions how to do it. But first he satisfied Ayisha by giving loud orders to every one to watch the man, and by telling her that he didn't care what she did with him after we reached Petra. Then, late in the afternoon, when Mujrim had rounded up the camels, a dispute was intentionally started about an old well, and whether a good trail to the southward did not make a circuit past it. The prisoner was asked, and he said he knew the well. Grim called him a father of lies, which he certainly was, and sent him off on the worst of the camels between Narayan Singh and me to prove his words. Ali Baba kept the Bishareen.

He led us a long way out into the desert among lumpy dunes in which the salt lay in strata, and where no sweet-water well could possibly be, or ever could have been. It was pretty obvious that all he wanted was a chance to escape from us, and he began offering bribes the minute we were out of sight of the camp.

The bribes were all in the nature of promises, however. He hadn't a coin or a thing except the clothes he wore, Ali Baba's gang having attended to that thoroughly.

"The wool-merchant--my master--is a rich man," he urged. "Let me go and he will be your friend for ever after."

"We have no need of friends," Narayan Singh answered. "This man and I, being spies in the government service, on the other hand, are men whose friendship is of value. You can serve us in a certain matter."

"Then give me money!" he retorted instantly. "He who serves the government nowadays receives pay."

"The way to receive pay," said I, "is to take this letter to the governor of Hebron, who will then know that a certain man is pretending to be Ali Higg. Thus you will do the government a great service, and may receive the difference in price between the Bishareen camel and that mean brute you ride now."

"We waste time. There is no well out here. Give me the letter!"

He was gone in a minute, headed straight for Hebron, and Narayan Singh and I fired several shots in the air to let Ayisha know what a desperate pursuit we had engaged in. When we rode into camp again, trying to look shamefaced, they had about finished packing up, so Grim had time to call us terrible names for Ayisha's benefit--names that it would not have been safe to apply to any of Ali Baba's men if he had chosen them for the job.

Those thieves would stand for any kind of devilry, and were willing to undertake all risks at Grim's bidding. Jail, fighting, hardship, meant to them no more than temporary inconvenience. But to have asked them to let a prisoner escape, and submit to shameful abuse for it afterward in the presence of a woman and strangers, would have been more than Arab loyalty could stand.

And, mother of me, how that woman Ayisha did revile us! If ever she had doubted we were Indians she was sure of it now. She swept with her tongue the whole three hundred million Indians into one vile horde and de-sexed, disinherited, declassed, and damned the lot of us. Before you think you know anything about abuse, wholesale or retail, you should hear a lady of the desert proclaim displeasure. I wouldn't be surprised to know that the very camels blushed.

It was all Narayan Singh could stand, for Ali Baba and his gang laughed derisively, and no true son of the East can endure to be laughed at.

"Let that mother of snakes beware!" he growled in my ear; and as it turned out in the end, he did not forget the grudge he owed her.

We were off again a good hour before sundown, and Mahommed Abbas sent out a screen of camel-men to follow us for several miles. They fired about twenty shots when we were well out of range, and boasted, as we learned afterward, of having put Ali Higg and a hundred men to rout.

But that did no harm. It reduced the real Ali Higg's prestige for a while all over the countryside; and in these days of League of Nations and mandates and whatnot it is hard enough in all conscience for brave villagers with muskets to find something to make up songs about. De Crespigny knew the truth about it as soon as our "escaped" man got to Hebron.

Before midnight we were well south of the Dead Sea and far beyond the border up to which the British mandate was supposed to be going to extend whenever the League of Nations Council should stop arguing. We were something like two thousand feet below sea-level now; but although the heat all day long under the tents had been almost intolerable, the night air was actually chilly because of the tremendous evaporation. The earth was throwing off the heat it had absorbed all day, and chill drafts crept from the mountaintops to take its place.

And as we crossed the imaginary border in pure, mellow moonlight, with our three bells clanging, you could have told its approximate whereabouts by the change that came over the gang. Even Grim's back, away ahead on the leading camel, assumed a jauntier swing. Old Ali Baba, next ahead of me, began to look ten years younger, and his sons and grandsons started singing--about Lot's wife acceptably enough, for we were near the fabled site of Sodom and Gomorrah, and the Prophet of Islam, who had nothing if not an eye for local color, incorporated that old story in the Koran.

The pillar of salt that used to be called Lot's wife, and that "stood there until this day," when the Old Testament writer penned his narrative, has fallen into the Dead Sea in recent memory. But all that did was to set loose imagination that had hitherto been tied to one landmark, and Ali Baba pointed out to me a dozen upright piles of argillaceous strata glistening in moonlight, every one of which he swore was either Lot's wife or one of her handmaidens.

"Such should be the fate of many other women," he asserted piously. "It would save a great deal of trouble."

The lady Ayisha heard that remark, and the things she said for the next ten minutes about men in general and old Ali Baba in particular were as poisonous as the brimstone that once rained down on Sodom and Gomorrah. She seemed to have no sense of being under obligation for the escort, but rather to think we were all in her debt for the privilege--a circumstance which appeared to me to bode ill for the manners of the gentry we proposed to visit.

Thereafter--I suppose since she considered she had utterly routed and reduced me to submission after the messenger's escape she summoned me to her side, thrusting the *shibrayah* curtains apart and beckoning with the fingers turned downward, Bedouin fashion. We conversed quite amicably for more than an hour, she mocking my Arabic pronunciation, but asking innumerable questions about India--who my mother was, for instance, and whether my father used to beat her much; what physic was used in India for date-boils; why I had not stayed at home; wasn't I afraid of meeting Ali Higg; and were there such great ones as he in India?

So, as there wasn't one chance in ten million of her knowing anything at all about India, I saw fit to explain that as a cockroach is to Allah so was Ali Higg to dozens of Indian bandits I had known. I told her tales of men's head piled mountains high, and of roads of corpses over which rajahs drove their chariots; of arenas full of tigers into which living prisoners were thrown once a week; and of a sheer cliff more than a mile high, over which women were tossed to alligators.

She took it all in, but doubted demurely at the end of it whether all those princely Indian terrorists added together could, as she put it, "reach to the middle of the thigh of Ali Higg"!

I asked her how she had come to marry the gentleman, and she answered with becoming pride that he had plundered her from the Bagdad caravan; but I think she meant by that a caravan of Bedouin on their way from Bagdad to wherever the grazing and thieving were good. She had a way of her own of enlarging things. Finally she asked me whether I carried good poison in my chest of medicines, and I told her I had some that could reach down to hell and kill the ifrits.

"Wallah!" she answered. "If you two eunuchs hadn't lost that prisoner we could have tested some of it on him!"

After that she dismissed me, I suppose that she might meditate on poison in the moonlight. I rode forward to take counsel with Grim, and some time during the night she got word with one of Ali Baba's younger sons. We had hardly camped an hour after dawn in the red-hot foothills east of the Dead Sea when Narayan Singh caught him rifling my chest, and he had the impudence to ask which were poisons and which not. Narayan Singh threatened an appeal to Grim, and the man apologized; but I saw Ayisha giving him sweetmeats in her tent not long afterward.

She had none of the ordinary Moslem woman's notions of privacy. A whole Bedouin family will live in a black tent ten by twelve, and though she had picked up wondrous ideas of high estate since her infancy, the desert upbringing remained. Her tent was pitched each day in the midst of ours, and she ordered every one about, Grim included, as if we were her husband's purchased slaves. And because it was Grim's idea to make use of her to gain access to her husband we all put up with it, fetching and carrying without a murmur--that is to say, all except one of us.

Whenever Narayan Singh had to do her bidding his great black beard rumbled with discontent; and as that only amused her she ordered him about more than any one, the others aiding and abetting by inventing things for him to be told to do. But it hardly paid her in the long run.

On the third day, when we camped by an old well that Ali Baba swore was the identical one made by the angel Gabriel to provide water for Hagar and Ishmael--there are twenty or thirty of those identical wells in Palestine alone, to say nothing of Arabia--she began to take a particular fancy to Grim and to treat him with more respect, giving him the title of prince on occasion, and abusing the men for not attending more swiftly to his needs.

Now, whatever the alleged custom of other lands may be--and I refuse to be committed on that point--there is no doubt whatever about the East. There it is the woman who makes the first advances. Grim took to sleeping in a tent with Mujrim and Ali Baba.

Considering the customs of that land--the savage, accepted way in which women swap owners when tribes are at war, and between times when the raids are made on caravan routes--it would be altogether wide of the mark to blame her too severely. Grim is a good-looking fellow, even in the khaki officer's uniform that makes most Christians look alike. Disguised as an Arab he takes the eye of any man, to say nothing of women.

The lines of his face are just deep enough to accent the powerful curve of his nose and chin; and his eyes, with their baffling color, arrest attention. Then he stands, too, in that gear like a scion of an ancient race, firmly, on strong feet, with his head held high and arms motionless--not fidgeting with one or both hands, as white men usually do. The wonder really is that Ayisha did not betray her designs on him sooner.

Narayan Singh grew as nervous as a hen in the presence of snakes, for he foresaw how Grim's star would surely wane from the moment any such woman as Ayisha should establish a claim on him; and he did not quite realize the full extent of Grim's resourcefulness in making the most of a situation. Old Ali Baba's advice, on the other hand, was just what he would have given to any of his sons.

"Let Ali Higg keep his wives within reach if he hopes to call them his! *Wallahi!* I would laugh to see the Lion of Petra tearing his clothes with rage for such a matter as this!"

And all the gang agreed.

Ayisha began to question Grim openly about his home and belongings. She wanted to know how many wives he had, and he told her none, which made her all the more determined. If he had affected squeamishness she would have despised him, and that would have been the end of her usefulness; for scorn is very close indeed to hate, and hate to spitefulness in the land where she was raised. But he did nothing of the sort. He was as frank as she was, and did his fencing, as you might say, with a club.

"The desert is full of women!" he told her on one occasion when she made more than usually open overtures.

"But not such as I am!"

"A woman's heart lies under her ribs, and who shall read it?" he answered.

"A pig can read some things!" she retorted; for he always managed to keep just clear of the point where frankness might have merged into poetry.

Her own four armed attendants seemed to take the whole affair rather speculatively. She was probably in position to have them crucified on her return to Petra in case they should offer unacceptable advice. And it may be they would have looked favorably on the chance to transfer allegiance from Ali Higg to Grim, who had crucified nobody yet; as Ayisha's servants they would doubtless go with her, should she change owners.

She asked me repeatedly for love potions, to be slipped into Grim's food or into his drink, and was so importunate about it that, after consulting Grim, I gave her some boric powder. The next morning Grim told her that her eyes were like a young gazelle's, so my reputation as a **hakim** rose several degrees.

"Is he mad?" growled Narayan Singh. "Ah, each man has his weakness! He and I have played with death a dozen times, but I never knew him lose his head. So he is woman-crazed? What next, I wonder!"

The girl had lots of encouragement, for, not counting the younger men, who were hell bent for any kind of mischief, and constantly egged her on, old Ali Baba spent half of each day in the tent expounding to Grim the ethics of such situations; and they were as simple as the code of Moses.

"Love thy neighbor's wife if she will let you. Defeat thy neighbor in all ways whenever possible. On these two hang all amusement and prosperity."

And Grim was much too wise to pretend to Ali Baba any other motive than expedience. It would not have paid to take the old rascal too much into his confidence, because most Arabs overplay their hand; but he did drop a hint or two; and from what he told me I should say it was Ayisha's persistent love-making that provided the first suggestion of a plan in his mind for bringing Ali Higg to terms.

But I'm sure the plan did not really take shape until we reached the sun-baked railway-line that drags its rusty length behind wild hills all the way from Damascus down to Mecca.

Some say that the very steel of the rails is sacred because it was built to carry pilgrims to the Prophet's tomb. But some say not. And those who lost the carrying trade on account of it, and the tribes that used to lie in wait in mountain-passes for the Damascus caravan in the month of pilgrimage, say distinctly not. Between these two opinions there is a third, that of the gentry who declare it is a curse, to be turned back on the heads of those who use it.

During four nights we climbed unlovely hills, avoiding villages--to the disgust of Ali Baba's gang, who would dearly have loved to pick a quarrel somewhere and loot. They had a thousand excuses for taking another trail, declaring that Grim had lost the way or would lose it; that there was sweeter water elsewhere; or that the hills were not so steep and hard on the camels. But the moon was nearly full by then, and Grim seemed to carry a map of the district in his head.

Whether he went by guesswork, or really knew, we turned up finally a few miles from El-Maan at the exact spot he had aimed for, and pitched camp soon after dawn within fifty yards of the track. There was no water in that place and the gang grumbled badly; but it was not long before the reason of his choice was fairly obvious.

Tracks across the desert have a way of curving from point to point, no more following a straight course than the cow-paths do in other lands. Where there is a rock, or some peculiar conformation of the ground to attract attention, men and beasts will head for it, attracted somewhat after the fashion of a compass-needle by a lodestone or lump of iron.

There was a rock shaped like a flattened egg beyond the track, two or three hundred yards away from us. It stood all alone in a dazzling wilderness that was doubtless green at certain seasons of the year, but now was bone-dry and glittering with flakes of mica. Close beside that ran a track worn by camels and horses, and the shadow of that great rock in a weary land was plainly a halting-place.

Our men wanted to cross over and take advantage of the shade it would give as the sun climbed higher, but Grim refused to let them; whereat Ayisha went into a shrewish rage, and ordered her four men to take up her tent and pitch it over by the rock whether Grim permitted it or not. So they obeyed her, and Grim said nothing.

The rest of us set about cooking breakfast after the morning prayers were over. My prayer-mat was next Narayan Singh's, and it was interesting to hear him curse the Prophet *sotto voce* while pretending to vie with those robbers in fervid protestations of faith in Islam. But more than the Prophet he cursed Ayisha, praying to his Hindu pantheon to wreak all wrath on her.

It was a diluted pantheon, of course, because he was a Sikh; he wasn't able to call on as many animal-shaped gods with as many arms and teeth as a Bengali could have urged into action; but he did his best with the technical resources at his disposal.

Without pretending to be a judge of other men's creeds, I thought at the time that he made a pretty workman-like hash of that lady's prospects, so far as his particular formula could do it. I jotted down some of his suggestions to the gods for future reference, and purpose to teach them to the U.S. Army mule-skinners next time this country goes to war.

While we were eating breakfast in a circle in front of the tents, all sticking our right hands into a common mess-pan and eating like wolves--you have to be awfully careful not to use your left hand, and unless you eat fast you'll get less than your share--there came five men on camels out of a wady--a shallow valley that lay like a cut throat with red rocks on its edge something over a mile away beyond the egg-shaped rock. They were armed--as everybody is in those parts who hopes to live--and in a hurry.

Ayisha and her people did not see them, because the great rock was in the way, but we left off eating to watch, and Grim went into his tent to use field-glasses without being seen. It is not unheard of for an Arab sheikh to use Zeiss binoculars, but it might make a stranger suspicious.

The five men came on at a gallop, sending up the dust in clouds like a cruiser's smoke-screen. They seemed to take it for granted that we were friends, for we were in full view and far outnumbered them, yet they did not check for an instant, and that in itself was a suspicious circumstance.

They came to a halt ten yards away from Ayisha's tent, and stared at her in silence, realizing, apparently for the first time, that they had come within rifle-shot of strangers. We could see her talking to them, but could not hear what she said. Perhaps that was as well. I think that even Grim with his poker face in perfect working order would have been flustered if he had been given time to think. The surprise, when it came, made him brace himself to meet it; and, once committed, he played with the sky for a limit as usual.

One thing was quite clear: Ayisha had made herself known to them, and they were properly impressed. They dismounted from their camels, and, after bowing to her as respectfully as any lord of the desert decently could do to a woman, they left their beasts kneeling and started all together toward us.

So Grim went out to meet them, even outdoing their measured dignity, striding as if the desert were his heritage. But he went only as far as the railway track, and waited; to have gone a step farther would have made them think themselves his superiors. Ali Baba, Mujrim, Narayan Singh, and I, went out and stood behind him at a properly respectful distance.

CHAPTER VI

"Him and Me--Same Father!"

Every detail of a man's bearing is watched carefully in that land. Every action has its value. The etiquette of the desert is more strict, and more dangerous to neglect, than that of palaces, although it is simpler and more to the point, being based on the instinct of self-preservation.

The Arabs who approached us, having ridden straight into a trap for all they knew, for they had expected friends and found strangers, were even more than usually observant of formality. They were fierce, fine-looking fellows, possessed of that dignity that only warfare with the desert breeds, and they saluted Grim with the punctilio of men who know the meaning of a fight to him who doubtless understands it too. A very different matter, that, to raising your Stetson on Broadway, with two cops on the corner and the Stars and Stripes floating from the hotel roof. They eyed Grim the while in the same sort of way that men who might be charged with trespass look at the game warden, waiting for him to speak first.

"Allah ysabbak bilkhair!" he rolled out at last.

"Allah y'a fik, ya Ali Higg!" they answered one after the other.

And then the oldest of them--a black-bearded stalwart with extremely aquiline nose and dark-brown eyes that fairly gleamed from under the linen head-dress, took on himself the role of spokesman.

"O Ali Higg! May Allah give you peace!"

"And to you peace!" Grim answered.

I could not see Grim's face, of course, since I stood behind him, but I did not detect the least movement of surprise or nervousness. He stood as if he were used to being called by that name, but the rest of us did not dare look at one another. Once across that railway-line we were in the real Ali Higg's preserves. It occurred to me at the moment as vastly safer to pose as the U.S. President in Washington.

Still, Grim had not actually accepted the situation yet. I held my breath, trying to remember to look like a product of Lahore University.

"We were on our way to El-Maan, O Ali Higg, not knowing that your honor had a hand in this affair."

"Since when is a lion not called a lion?" demanded Grim. "Who gave thee leave to name me?"

"Pardon, O Lion of Petra! But the woman yonder, boasting with proper pride that she is Your Honor's wife, bade us approach and pay respect."

On my left I heard Narayan Singh muttering obscenities through set teeth. On the right old Ali Baba wore a twinkle in a wicked eye; the rest of his face was as emotionless as the face of the desert; but when an old man is amused not even the crow's-feet can do less than advertise the fact.

"A woman's tongue is like a camel bell," said Grim. "It clatters unceasingly, and none can silence without choking it. But art thou a woman?"

"Pardon, O Lion of Petra!"

There followed a long pause. When men meet in the desert it is only those from the West who are in any hurry to betray their business. There being an infinity of time, that man is a liar who proclaims a shortage of it.

"Will the sun not rise tomorrow?" asks the East.

Grim stood like a statue; and, judging by my own feelings, who had nothing at all to do but look on, I should say that was a test of strength.

"Last week the train was punctual at El-Maan--three hours after sunrise," said the spokesman at last.

On lines where there is only one train a week it is not unusual for its arrival to be the chief social event on the country-side, but that hardly seemed to me to account for the way those five men had been driving their camels. However, as Grim knew no more of their business than the rest of us, and needed desperately to find out, he was careful to ask no questions.

No desert responds to the inquisitive folk who camp on its edge and demand to be told; but it will tell you all it knows if you keep quiet and govern yourself in accordance with its moods. The men who live in the desert are of the same pattern-

-fierce, hot, cold, intolerant, cruel, secretive, given to covering their tracks, and yet not without oases that are better than much fine gold to the man who knows how to find them. They enjoy a proverb better than some other men like promises.

"Allah marks the flight of birds. Shall He not decree a train's journey?" said Grim.

"Inshallah, Lion of Petra! The train will come, when that is written, and that which is written shall befall. It is said there are sons of corruption on the train, who bear much wealth with them.

"It were a pity to leave all the looting to those who got to El-Maan soonest. They who slay will claim the booty.

"Or does Your Honor intend to arrive afterward and claim a share, leaving the labor to those who seek labor? In that case we crave permission to join Your Honor's party. It may be we can help enforce Your Honor's just demands, and be recompensed accordingly?"

"Wallahi!" Grim answered after a long pause. "Who sets himself to plunder trains without my leave? Have I been such short time in Petra that men doubt who rules here? Have I not said the train shall pass El-Maan and come thus far? Who dares challenge me? Do I wait here for nothing? Shall I be satisfied with a string of empty cars?"

The Arab turned and conferred for a moment with his four friends. They shook their heads.

"O Lord of the Desert," he said after a minute, "none has heard of this decree. Your Honor's messenger may have failed or have fallen into bad hands on the way. Word has not come that you reserve this train for your own profit. There will be fifty men at El-Maan now waiting to slay certain passengers and plunder others."

Grim had evidently made up his mind and had set full sail on the course indicated. I confess I shuddered at the prospect; but I never saw a man look more pleased than Ali Baba, and Narayan Singh's face betrayed militant admiration. Nor have I ever heard such a streak of fulminous bad language as Grim swore then, calling earth and all its elements to witness the brimstone anger of a robber chief.

"Go ye," he thundered, "and tell those sons of swine that I say the train shall pass to this point. And as to what happens thereafter that is my affair. Bid any and all who chose to dispute my word to look first to their wives and goods. I have spoken."

The five men fell back a pace in consternation, no doubt partly affected for the sake of flattery; but they were quite obviously disconcerted.

"Wallahi! If we go on such an errand who shall save our lives? Who are we to come between wolves and their prey?"

"Say ye are my messengers," retorted Grim. "Let any touch a messenger of mine who dares."

"But they will not believe us."

"That is their affair. It is Allah's way to make blind those who it is written are to be destroyed."

"Nay, Lion of Petra, give a man to go with us--one whom they will know and recognize. Then all shall be well."

Have I ever said that Grim is a genius? He can take longer chances in a crisis with a more unerring aim than any man I ever knew. Surely he took one then.

"Nay," he laughed. "I will send them a woman. Let us see who will dare gainsay the woman."

That was simply supreme genius. It even pleased Narayan Singh, since the tables were turned on Ayisha. The only reason she could possibly have had for telling these men that Grim was Ali Higg was to score off him, either by capturing him for herself, or in the alternative by ruining him for rejecting her advances. It was not clear yet which of the two she hoped to accomplish; perhaps, little savage that she was, she would have been content with either alternative and had simply chosen to force the issue.

At any rate Grim had passed the buck back to her. He sent me over to the rock to fetch her, and I found her smiling serenely, like the Sphinx, only with more than a modicum of added mischief.

"Woman, the Lion of Petra summons you," said I.

She laughed at that as if the world were at her feet--got up, and stretched herself, and yawned like a lazy cat that sees the milk being set down in a saucer--straightened her dress, and nodded knowingly to her four men. She had evidently reached an understanding with them.

"I hasten to do my lord's bidding," she answered, and followed me back.

It calls for all your presence of mind to remember to walk in front of a woman who is addressed as often as not as princess; but if I had walked behind her they would have suspected me at once of being no true Moslem.

I returned and stood behind Grim, and she stood in front of him, so that I was able to see her face. It was as good as a show to see her swallow back surprise and wonder at him open-eyed, as he played the part she had foisted on him and loaded her with the responsibility.

"Go with these men, Ayisha, and tell those swine at El-Maan that I say the train shall pass unharmed as far as this point. Moreover, say that none may trespass. What shall take place here is my affair. The range of my rifle is the measure of the line across which none may come.

"Stay with them, Ayisha, until the train leaves El-Maan. Then you may leave your camel and return hither on the train. That is my order."

She was bluffed. And she recognized it with a sort of dog-like glance of admiration. We had all her baggage, for one thing, and it represented more wealth than any Bedouin woman would let go willingly.

Now if she were to reverse what she had said, and refuse to advertise Grim as Ali Higg, these five men and probably others would surely denounce her to her real husband. She had no choice. But she was sharp-witted, and made the most of the situation even so.

"Shall I go alone, my lord? Alone with these strangers?"

"Take two of your servants."

But what she wanted to make sure of was that Grim might not decamp with her baggage and leave her to face the consequences. It seems you can fall in love in the desert without putting too much faith in masculine nature.

"Nay, give me two men I can trust. Give me that and that one."

She selected old Ali Baba and me; and it was a shrewd choice, for unless Grim was a more than usually yellow-minded rascal he was surely not going to leave the captain of his gang behind. And no doubt she supposed I was valuable to Grim because of the friendly, confidential way in which he always treated me. In other words, she proposed to have two first-class hostages.

Grim gave her three. He sent Ali Baba, me, and Mujrim, and mounted her on the Bishareen dromedary, that men might know she was one whom her lord delighted to honor. She tried to get a chance to whisper to him, but he was too alert and acted exactly as if he had known her all his life, needing no explanations or assurances.

So off we nine rode beside the railway track, she leading, since she was chief emissary, and the last I saw of Grim for a few hours he was squatting in the circle of remaining men, talking to them as calmly as if nothing had happened.

Well, there was nothing for me to do but ride forward and watch points. I was a hostage without responsibility.

If Ayisha should chose to turn on us and hand me over to the crowd at El-Maan I believed I would have wit enough to denounce her in return; and it might be that as a Darwaish I could claim immunity. Failing that, I found myself able to hope with a really acute enthusiasm that my shrift at the crowd's hands might be short. I did not want to be crucified, or pulled in pieces by camels; but if mine was to be the casting vote, of the two the camels had it.

There were other points to be considered. I had a rifle slung behind me, and two bandoliers. However, it was highly unlikely I would have a chance to use the rifle, which is an awkward weapon at close quarters when surrounded.

But hidden under my coat I had two repeating-pistols and a knife. Since a man can't prevent himself from making plans when there is nothing else to think about, I made up my mind finally in case of trouble to let them take the rifle and the knife; they might then suppose me to be disarmed. After that, if the trouble should be due to Ayisha's treason, I would execute her, and shoot myself in the head with the same pistol rather than submit to torture.

At the end of the first mile I drew alongside Ali Baba and passed him my second pistol. It did not seem any of my business to advise him what to do with it beyond hiding it under his clothes. The old rascal's eyes glittered as his hand closed on it, and it seemed to me he understood; and so he did, but not what I intended.

I never got the pistol back. He understood that a fool and his repeater are soon parted. When I asked him for it afterward he vowed he had lost it, and called his son Mujrim in addition to Allah and Mohammed and all the saints to witness that he spoke virgin truth, and, moreover, that he never lied, and would rather die ten times over than play a trick on me. I have heard since that he has become a very good shot with a repeating-pistol, but has difficulty in stealing suitable ammunition.

Ayisha wasted no breath on conversation on the way, but whipped her camel to its utmost speed after the first mile, so that we had our work cut out to keep up with her. It is aggravating to ride a big beast and try in vain to overtake a little one; but she had been born to the game, and there wasn't a man in the party who could have won a race against her, whichever of the animals she rode; for the camel knows quicker than a horse whether his rider understands the art or not. And art it is, as surely as painting or music--art that can be tediously learned in a degree, but must be born in you if you are ever to excel at it.

The desert was all red sand now and dreary beyond human power to imagine. The clouds of dust we kicked up followed us, and even the cloths we kept across our mouths and nostrils did not keep it out. You felt like a mummy riding a race in hell, and how the camels managed to breathe I can't guess. The sun on our right hand was just at the angle where it struck your eyes under the *kuffiyi.*

But I was the only one who seemed at all distressed by any of those inconveniences; the others accepted them as in the natural order of things, and my camel, realizing how I felt, galloped last in the worst of the dust.

El-Maan itself was a picture of green trees above a mud wall; but we did not visit it, for the station, with its hideous red water-tanks, was a mile and a half to the eastward of the place--a miserable, bleak, unpainted iron roof and buildings, with a place alongside that had once been a Greek hotel.

At present it looked like a camel-mart; but there were dozens of horses there too, gaudily turned out like the camels with red worsted trimmings on saddles and bridles. And as for the fifty men our five new acquaintances had spoken of, there were a hundred and fifty if one, all herded in groups, each with a rifle over his arm or slung across his shoulder. Their talk ceased as we rode along the track, and those who were on the platform--about half of them--eyed Ayisha with as much curiosity as a Bedouin taken by surprise ever permits himself to betray.

She did not give them much time for reflection, and wasted none whatever on conciliation, but affronted them from camel-back, having learned that method, no doubt, from her rightful lord and master. It was obvious from the first that they all knew her by sight.

"Wallahi! Good meat for the crows ye will all be presently! Has the Lion of Petra lost his teeth that jackals hunt ahead of him? Did the men of Dat Ras profit by

coming between him and his prey? Go, look at Rat Das and count the splinters of men's bones! So shall your bones lie--ye who tempt the wrath of Ali Higg!"

She rode along the line, showing her little teeth like pomegranate seeds in a sneer that would have made a passport clerk take notice; and her voice was raised to a shrill, harpy scream that rasped under the iron roof, so that none could have pretended he did not hear.

"The Lion claims this train! The Lion of Petra lies in wait for it at a place of his own choosing! Who dares forestall him? Who dares slay one passenger, or loot one truck? Who dares? Stand out, whoever dares, that I may take his name back to the Lion of Petra!"

Nobody did stand out. They all herded closer together, as if in fear that any one left on the edge of the crowd might be assumed to challenge her authority. Yet they looked capable of plundering a city, that company of stately cutthroats. Perhaps some of them had seen what actually happened when Ali Higg raided Dat Ras. Certainly they came from scattered settlements, on which Ali Higg could take detailed vengeance whenever it suited him.

"Ye know me! I wait here for the train. I shall ride on it to where the Lion of Petra waits. Who dares interfere with me or follow? Let him name himself! Who dares?"

Her savagery fed itself on threats, and increased as she felt herself grow mistress of the situation. Partly the primitive love of power, partly the animal instinct to subject and oppress--pride on top of that, and something of her sex, too, glorying in giving orders to the self-styled sterner members--drove her to increasing frenzy.

And it was not fear alone that impressed the crowd and impelled it to obedience, for those highland Bedouins are, after all, too practical for that. We were but nine all told, to their seven or eight score, and they might have enforced the logic of that first, and left the threatened consequences for afterward, but for the appeal of the spectacular.

It bewildered them to be harangued confidently by a woman--they who were used to watching women carry loads. There was something revolutionary about it that took their breath away, and swept their own determination into limbo.

As always, the men in the background, who felt they could avoid recognition, were the only ones who ventured to raise objection. One or two of them started to laugh, that being the best answer all the world over to any threat, and if the laugh had spread that would likely have been the end of us. I had unslung my rifle and held it in full view resting on my thigh, being minded to look as murderous as possible, but she stole all my thunder by suddenly snatching the rifle away and drawing back its bolt to cock the spring with that almost effortless adroitness that comes of long use.

"Who laughs at the Lion of Petra's threat?" she screamed, raising herself in the saddle to survey the crowd. "Who laughs? He shall die by the hand of a woman! Who laughs, I say?"

But nobody wanted to die by a woman's hand; and nobody chose to slay the woman, because of the certainty of vengeance dealt by an expert in terrorism. I know I didn't doubt she would have used the rifle, and I don't suppose they did. If she couldn't be laughed out of countenance the only alternative was bloodshed, and none dared show fight.

Old Ali Baba worked his camel closer, and, because an Arab must boast at every opportunity, began to whisper in my ear.

"*Wallahi!* Was I not wise? It was I who told her if she wanted our Jimgrim she should tell the world she is his wife and he the veritable Ali Higg! It takes an old man's tongue to guide the cleverest woman!"

The train screamed then in the distance, and a Syrian station agent in tattered khaki uniform went through the wholly unnecessary process of letting down a signal. We got off the track and rode our camels round on to the platform. The crowd gave way before us, and Ayisha thrust herself this and that way among them, breaking up groups, striking me over the wrist with the stick she had for flogging the camel because I tried to regain the rifle.

By the time the rusty, creaking, groaning rattletrap of a train drew up there was not an element of cohesion left in the crowd. She knew too much to drive them away to where they might have regained something of determination, but let them stand there under her eye where they could see in herself the ruthless symbol of Ali Higg's ruthlessness. And not even the sight of the frightened passengers, in a panic because of tales that had been told them up the line, could restore their plunder-lust.

As a matter of fact that was a romantic little mixed train when you come to think of it. The Arab engine-driver, piloting his charge through no-man's land, where the bones of former train crews lay bleaching, simply because he was an engine-driver and that was his job; the freight in locked steel cars consigned by optimists who hoped it might reach its destination; the four guards armed with worn-out rifles that they did not dare use; the four passenger-cars with their window-glass all shot away; the half-dozen Arab artisans carried along for makeshift repairs en route; and the more than brave--the too-fatalist-to-care-much passengers wondering which of their number had an enemy at every halting-place; and along with that the formalism--the observance of conventions such as blowing the whistle and pulling down the signal, on a track that carried one train one way once a week; it made you feel like taking off your hat to it all, reminding me in a vague way of those Roman legionaries who kept up the semblance of their civilization after the power of Rome had waned.

I rode over beside the engine-driver and warned him to pull out before trouble started. But he had to take in water first. And he seemed to be an expert in symptoms of lawlessness. Leaning his grimy head and shoulders out of the cab, he looked the crowd over, spat, and showed his yellow teeth in a grin that vaguely reminded me of Grim's good-humored smile.

"Mafish!" he remarked, summing up the situation in two syllables. "Nothing doing!"

I would have given, and would give now, most of what I own for that man's ability to pass such curt, comprehensive judgment without reservation, equivocation, or hesitation. I rather suspect that it can only be learned by sticking to your job when the rest of the world has been fooled into thinking it is making history out of talk and treason.

There was nothing whatever but water for the train to wait for. Nobody had business at El-Maan, for the simply sufficient reason that you can't do business where governments don't function, where all want everything for nothing, and whoever could pay won't.

The engine-driver's grimier assistant swung the water-spout clear and climbed back over the cab, cursing the view, crowds, coal-dust, prospect--everything. He meant it too. When he said he wished the devil might pitch me into hell and roast me forever he wasn't exaggerating. But I got off my camel and boarded the engine nevertheless. Ayisha had handed over her mount to Ali Baba and entered the caboose, ignoring the protests of the uniformed conductor who, having not much faith in fortune, did not care whom he offended. But he might as well have insulted a camel as Ayisha, for all he would have gained by it.

My friend the engine-driver blew the whistle; somebody on the platform tooted a silly little horn; a signal descended in the near distance and we started just as I caught sight of Mujrim coming to take my camel.

Then it occurred to some bright genius that even if they might not loot the train there was no embargo on rejoicing; and there was only one way to do that. What they saw fit to rejoice about I don't know, but one shot rang in the air, and a second later fifty bullets pierced the dinning iron roof.

That made such a lovely noise and so scared the passengers that they could not resist repeating it, and by the time we had hauled abreast of the distance-signal there was not much of the roof left.

I saw Ali Baba and Mujrim take advantage of the excitement to start back with the camels; and two minutes later about twenty men decided to follow them at a safe distance. The rest had begun to scatter before the train was out of sight, and I never again saw one of the five gentry who had introduced us to the whole proceedings.

Then my friend the engine-driver found time to be a little curious.

"What'n hell?" he asked, in the *lingua franca* that all Indians are supposed to understand.

So I answered him in the mother argot at a venture, and he bit.

"There's a man down the line a piece who'll blow your train to hell," said I, "unless you pull up when he flags you."

"Son of a gun, eh?"

"Sure bet!"

"Where you learn English?"

"States," said I. "You been there too?"

"Sure pop! Goin' back some time."

"Not if you don't stop her when you get the hint, you won't. That guy down there ahead means business."

I don't think he would have dared try to run the gauntlet in any case, for the best the engine could do with that load behind it was a wheezy twenty miles an hour, and the track was so out of repair that even that speed wasn't safe. I was willing to bet Grim hadn't lifted a rail or placed any obstruction in the way, but the driver had no means of knowing that.

"Son of a gun, eh?" he repeated. "What in 'ell's 'e want?"

"Nothing, if you pay attention to him. All he hankers for is humoring. He wants to talk."

"Uh! What in 'ell's a matter with him?"

"Nothing, but he'll put a crimp in your machinery unless you stay and chin with him."

"I give him dry steam. He'll run like the devil."

"Don't you believe it. He's wise. Better humor him."

"Shucks! I shoot him. I shot lots o' men."

"No need to shoot," said I. "This is love stuff. He's got a lady in the last car."

"Oh, gal on the train, eh? All right. You climb back along the cars an' kick her off soon as you see him."

"Gosh! I'd sooner kick a nest of hornets!"

"You her brother?"

"Not so's you'd notice it."

"What then?"

"She's got my gun. Barring that we're not real close related."

"Uh! Those damned Bedouin fellers can't shoot for nuts. Let 'em fire away. I take a chance."

"Ever hear of Ali Higg?" I asked him.

He turned his head from peering down the blistering hot track, wiped the sweat from his face and hands with a filthy rag, and looked at me keenly.

"Why? You know him?"

"Yes. I asked if you do."

"Son of a gun! Him and me--same father!"

"You mean he's your brother?"

He nodded.

"He's the man you've got to pull up for."

"His gal on the train?"

"Sure thing."

He resumed his vigil, leaning over the side of the engine with one hand on the throttle-lever.

"All right," he said. "I stop for him. Son of a gun! If he bust my train I kill the sucker!"

I never posed as much of a diplomatist, but it seemed wise to me in the circumstances not to offer any further information or ask questions. But I was curious. It was possible that Ali Higg's brother had been given the task of running that train for the reason that no lesser luminary would have one chance in a thousand of reaching the destination.

I never found out whether my guess was right or not, and never left off rating that engine-driver in any case as one of the world's heroes. I've a notion there is a book that might be written about him and his train.

A polished black dot in the distance soon increased into the flattened egg-shaped rock, and then we saw Grim standing on the track with all his men.

That is the safest place to stop a train from, because you avoid a broadside from the car-windows. True to his word the driver came to a standstill, and Grim came up to speak with him just as I jumped off. I waited, expecting to see a contretemps.

"Ya Ali Higg! You fool!" said the driver. "You would kill your own brother? You let me go!"

"Hah! You recognize me, then?" said Grim, coolly enough on the surface.

But his poker mask was off. In that land of polygamy and deportations it is frequent enough that one brother does not know the other by sight; but it must be disconcerting, all the same, to have a supposititious brother sprung on you. He gave a perceptible start, as he had not done when first addressed as Ali Higg that day.

"Mashallah!" swore the driver. "I would know thine evil face with the meat stripped off it! Nevertheless, thou and I are brothers and this is my train. So let me go!"

Grim watched Ayisha jump out of the caboose with my rifle in her hand, and turn to take aim at the open door, through which the conductor's voice came croaking blasphemy.

"All right," he said. "Since thou and I are brothers, go thy way! *Allah ysall-*

mak!"

The driver did not wait for a second hint, but shoved the lever over so hard that the wheels spun and the whole train came within an ace of bucking off the track. And before the caboose had passed us Ayisha was alongside Grim abusing him for not having broken the locks off the steel freight-cars.

"I am a robber's wife!" she said, stamping her foot indignantly. "What sort of robber are you that let such loot pass free?"

"Shall I rob my mother's son?" Grim asked her. "God forbid!"

Then he turned to me, wondering.

"Can you beat it?" he said.

CHAPTER VII

"You Got Cold Feet?"

We did not have to wait long for Ali Baba, Mujrim, and the camels, for they had not been fools enough to dawdle, with a hundred and fifty balked freebooters within rifle-shot, whose resilient pride was likely to breed anger. You can't lead camels any more than horses as fast as you can ride them; unless stampeded they tow loggily; but the fact that two or three dozen mounted Arabs had elected to follow along behind and watch from a safe distance what might happen to the train had lent Ali Baba wings.

And the same fact gave us wings too. We were up and away at once, headed eastward toward Petra, I perched on top of a baggage beast until Ali Baba could cut across at an angle and overtake us.

So those who watched no doubt confirmed the story of Ali Higg's presence on the scene. Had they not from the horizon seen the train stopped? Did they not with their own eyes see us scoot for Petra? And who else than the redoubtable Ali Higg would be likely to own such a string of splendid camels--he who could take what he coveted, and never coveted anything except the best?

The evidence of identity was strong enough for a judge and jury. Men have been hanged in America on less.

But that didn't help make the rest of our course any clearer than a fog off Sandy Hook. The real Ali Higg was in Petra like a dragon in a cave, and from all accounts of him he was not the sort of gentleman likely to lavish sweet endearments on a rival who had stolen not only his thunder, but his name as well.

"When in doubt go forward" is good law; but which is forward and which backward when you stand in the middle of a circle of doubt is a point that invites argument; and as soon as I could get my own camel I rode up beside Grim to find out whether our leader had a real plan or was only guessing.

But he seemed in no doubt at all, only satisfied, with the air of a scientist who has at last found the key to a natural puzzle. I found him chuckling.

"That explains a hundred things," he said.

"What does?"

"Why, my likeness to Ali Higg. It's evidently so. I've often been kept awake wondering why strangers--Bedouins mostly--would show me such deference until they found out who I really am, and after that would have to be handled without gloves. It bothered me. It looked as if I had some natural gift that I couldn't identify, and that got smothered as soon as I put mere brains to work.

"But I see now; they mistook me for the robber, and the reaction when they found out I was some one less like the devil made them act like school-kids who think they can guy the teacher. Now I understand, I'll do better."

"The point is," said I, "that you're established as the robber now, and here we are riding straight for his den. Can we fight him and his two hundred?"

"Fighting is a fool's game ten times out of nine," he answered. "That's to say, it's always a fool who starts the fight. The wise man waits until fighting is the only resource that's left to him."

"Why not wait, then, and watch points?"

"Because we're not dealing with a wise man; he's only clever and drastic. If we wait word's bound to reach him that some one's posing as himself, and he'll sally forth to make an example of us--do a good job of it too!

"I'd hate to be caught out in the desert with twenty men by Ali Higg! He's a rip-roaring typhoon. But the worst typhoon the world ever saw had a soft spot in the middle.

"You know what the Arab say? `A dog can scratch fleas, but not worms in his belly!' We've got to be worms in the belly of Ali Higg, and where the man is there will be his belly also. We've got to stage what the movie people call a close-up."

Almost every one in the outfit had a different view of the situation, although all agreed that Grim was the man to stay with. Narayan Singh, growling in my ear incessantly, scented intrigue, and his Sikh blood tingled at the thought; he began to look more tolerantly on Ayisha as a mere instrument whom Grim would find some chance of using.

"For the cleverest woman whom the devil ever sent to ruin men is after all but a lie that engulfs the liar. I know that man Jimgrim. She will dig a pit, but he will not fall into it. It may be that we shall all die together, but what of that?"

Ayisha, on the other hand, was getting nervous. Grim avoided her. She was reduced to questioning others, edging the little Bishareen alongside each in turn. She seemed no longer able to suffer the close confinement of the *shibriyah,* but endured the scorching sun and desert flies with less discomfort than the rest of us betrayed, camels included.

"What will he do? Is he mad? Does he think that the Lion of Petra is a camel to be managed with a rope and a stick?

"I have given him his chance; because of my words men already fear him. Why doesn't he plunder, then, and run to his own home? Why doesn't he talk with me and let me tell him what to do next? I know all these people--all their villages--everything!"

"All women know too much, yet never what is needful," Ali Baba answered.

He was frankly jubilant. Son and grandson of robbers by profession, father and grandfather of educated thieves, life meant lawlessness to him, and he could see nothing but honest pleasure and the chance of profit in Grim's predicament. He loved Grim, as all Arabs do love the foreigner who understands them, deploring nothing except that unintelligible loyalty to a Western code of morals that according to Ali Baba's lights consisted of pure foolishness. And now, as he saw it, Grim stood committed to a course that could only lead to trickery. And all trickery must pave the way for plunder. And plundering was fun.

His sons and grandsons in varying degree saw matters from the old man's viewpoint, although, having had rather less experience of it, they were not quite so confident of Grim's generalship; but they made up for that by perfectly dog-like devotion to "the old man, their father," whose word and whose interpretation of the Koran was the only law they knew.

What tickled their fancy most was Ali Baba's cleverness in egging on Ayisha to advertise Grim as Ali Higg. Again and again on the march that day, in spite of the grilling heat, and thirst and flies, they burst into roars of laughter over it, chaffing Ayisha's four men unmercifully.

And after a while Mahommed, the youngest of Ali Baba's sons, regarded by all the others as the poet of the band and therefore the least responsible and most to be humored in his whims, made up a song about it all. It called for something more than boisterous spirits; it needed the fire of enthusiasm and ingrained pluck to set them all singing behind him in despite of the desert heat and the dazzling, bleak, unwatered view. They sang the louder in defiance of the elements.

"Lord of the desert is Ali Higg!
Akbar! Akbar![18]
Lord of the gardens of grape and fig.
Akbar! Akbar!
Lord of the palm and clustered date.
Mishmish,[19] olive and water sate
Hunger and thirst in Ali's gate!
Akbar! Akbar! Akbar Ali Higg!

"Lion of lions and lord of lords!
Akbar! Akbar!
Chief of lances, prince of swords!
Akbar! Akbar!
Red with blood is the realm he owns!
Bzz-u-wzz-uzz the blood-fly drones!
Crack-ak-ak-ak! The crunching bones!
Akbar! Akbar! Akbar Ali Higg!
    "Jackals feed on Ali's trail!
Akbar! Akbar!
Speed and strength and numbers fail!
Akbar! Akbar!
Swooping along in a cloud of sand,

---

18 Akbar means "great."
19 Mishmish--apricot. In that land of drought and desolation the highest compliment you can pay a man is to call him lord of water and ripening fruit.

Killing and conquering out of hand
 Hasten the slayers of Ali's band!
Akbar! Akbar! Akbar Ali Higg!

"Camel and horse and fat-tail sheep,
Akbar! Akbar!
Ali's kite-eyed herdsmen keep!
Akbar! Akbar!
Gold and silver and gems of the best,
Amber and linen and silks attest
 What are the profits of Ali's quest!
Akbar! Akbar! Akbar Ali Higg!

"Fair are the fortunes of Ali's men!
Akbar! Akbar!
Each has slave-women eight or ten!
Akbar! Akbar!
Ho! Where the dust of the desert swirls
Over the plain as his cohort whirls,
Oho! the screams of the plundered girls!
Akbar! Akbar! Akbar Ali Higg!"

There was any amount more of it, but most of the rest was not polite enough for print, because the Arab likes to enter into details. It sounded much better in Arabic, anyhow. And more and more frequently as the song grew lurid and they warmed to the refrain they made their point by changing the third Akbar into Jimgrim:

"Akbar! Akbar! Jimgrim Ali Higg!"

It suited their sense of humor finely to announce to the wind and the kites that Grim, the strict, straight, ethical American was a ravisher of virgins and a slitter of offenseless throats, who knew no mercy--a man without law in this world or prospect of peace in the next.

When we reached an oasis about noon--sweet water and thirty or forty palm-trees--and simply had to camp there because the camels were exhausted after a night and half a day of strenuous marching, they were still so full of high spirits that they had to work them off somehow; and unwittingly I provided the excuse.

I was on the lee side of a camel, opening a boil in Mujrim's leg with his razor, when I caught sight of one of the younger men trying to burgle the medicine-chest. I yelled at him, and naturally gashed my patient's leg, who rose in giant wrath and with enormous fairness smote the real culprit.

The resulting blasphemous bad language brought Ali Baba to the scene at once as peacemaker, with all the gang behind him; and in a minute they had all joined hands, with Mahommed standing in the center, and were dancing like a lot of pouter-pigeons, singing a new song about Mujrim's leg, and a razor, and blood on the sand, and palm-trees, and a saint, and my superhuman ability to let daylight into the very heart of boils. You don't have to believe any one who tells you that Arabs haven't humor.

There were the ruins of half a dozen mud-walled huts near the spring in that oasis. There had once been a sort of rampart and a gate, but there was hardly enough of that left to show where it stood. The only building still quite intact was a stone tomb of about the height of a man, with a plastered cupola roof; and Ali Baba, who always knew everything, swore that was a great saint's grave, and that there was much virtue and good luck to be gained by praying inside the tomb. So they all took turns to go in and pray fervently--two-bow prayers as they called them--reciting thereafter such scripture as Ali Baba thought suitable and could remember.

Hunting about in the ruins I found indubitable human bones. Ayisha, when asked about it, said that Ali Higg had raided the place several months ago and killed or captured every one.

"Because he is lord of the waters," she explained, and seemed to think that reason unassailable.

There was quite a dispute at that place as to who should stand first guard while the rest of us slept, but Grim settled it by casting lots with date-stones in a way that was new, but that seemed to satisfy every one--especially as the first watch fell to Narayan Singh and me.

"That is because the rest of us said our prayers," explained Ali Baba piously.

But I think it was really because Grim knew how to play tricks with the date-stones.

The Sikh and I kept making the circuit of the palm-trees and talking to keep each other from getting too sleepy, for there is no time when desire to sleep so loads you down as in the noon heat after a long march. You very often can't sleep then because of the very heat that makes you drowsy; but the glare has been so trying to your eyes that you yearn to shut them, and inertia sits on your spine and shoulders like a load of lead.

"Thou and I must watch that woman, sahib," said Narayan Singh. "Our Jimgrim will make use of her; but how shall he do that if her heart changes? As long as she hopes to snare him I am not afraid of her. But what if it should be she who grows afraid as we get nearer to Ali Higg's nest? A woman afraid is worse than a man with a dagger in the dark. Suppose she bolts to Ali Higg and lays information against us--what then?"

I tried to argue him out of his anxiety, because I wanted to sleep when my turn came. My habit of never looking for trouble is a lovely one until trouble starts; but the Sikh, being only a heathen, could not be persuaded; so I had to promise him that, turn about, four hours on and four off, he and I would watch Ayisha faithfully until such time as Grim should make other disposition of our services or there should be no more need.

"And I think, sahib, that it will be best to shoot or stab her without argument if she turns treacherous."

But I never stabbed or shot a woman yet. I have a loose-kneed prejudice against it. I said so.

"Then, sahib, if it be your turn on watch, and you detect treachery, summon me, and I will send her to *Jehannum.*"[20]

"I think we ought to speak to Jimgrim about it," I objected. "He might have other plans."

The Sikh turned that over in his mind during one whole circuit of the palm-trees, stroking his great beard with his right hand the while as if the friction would inspire his brain.

---

20   Hell

"Jimgrim will say she is a woman and therefore must not be killed in any event," he answered at last. "But that is of the nature of his error, all men suffering delusion in some form, since none is perfect. If we submit the problem to him he will answer wrongly; but we shall then have received orders, which, as faithful men, we must not disobey.

"As concerns ourselves, being men without specific orders on that point, the question is simple: Of that woman and that man, if the one must live and the other die, which shall it be? And I say Jimgrim shall live, if I die afterward even by his hand for it."

It sounded logical. The arguments with which an unselfish, honest fellow deceives himself into wrong-doing always do bear quite a lot of investigation. But I was at sea before the mast once, where I learned painfully that the captain commands the ship; not even the notions of the buckiest bucko mate amount to as much as a barnacle's bootlace if the old man disagrees from them.

"What makes you think he doesn't understand the obvious danger of Ayisha?" said I.

"No man from the West ever understood a woman of the East," he answered.

That being obviously true--Adam did not understand Eve, and no man from anywhere has understood any woman since--I had to rack my brains for a different argument.

"There are two sure ways of discovering treason," I said at last. "One way is to pick a quarrel with the person you suspect. But the safer way is to seem very friendly.

"Now--why don't you make love to her? You're a fine, big, handsome man. I don't suppose she'll prefer you in her heart to Jimgrim, but she'll not be ashamed to appear to respond, and if she has evil intentions she will surely seek to take advantage of your passion to forward her own plans. Seeking to make use of you, she will betray herself."

"So speaks the jackal to the tiger. 'This way, sahib! That way, sahib! A broad-horned sambhur to be killed, worthy of your honor's strength!' Why don't you make love to her?"

"Because I'm afraid," said I quite frankly. "If I thought I could get away with it I'd try. But she'd laugh at me, whereas your attentions might flatter her."

"You think so?"

He stroked his great beard again, and twisted his mustache.

"I'm sure of it."

"Atcha. We shall see. I will give the trollop that one chance. It may be she will preserve her head on her shoulders yet by confiding in me; for if I can forewarn Jimgrim of her plans I will reckon it beneath my dignity to use a sword on her. So. It is settled. We shall see."

You know that warm glow of vanity that sweeps over you when another fellow concedes your plan to be better than his? It is rather like the effect of certain drugs--a highly agreeable sensation while it lasts.

But it was tempered in my case by that reference he had made to a jackal, and I'm still left wondering how much justice there was in the insinuation. Narayan Singh and I are friends right down to this minute, but I am none the less conscious of a query that seems to spoil confidence a little.

He, being master of himself by training, and used to sleeping when he saw fit, volunteered to take the first four-hour watch on Ayisha, so I got as much sleep as the flies and the snores of the rest of the gang would permit, and awoke toward evening to the sound of unaccustomed voices outside my tent. There was one voice with a squeak in it like a rusty wheel that I had certainly never heard before.

It seemed we had made some prisoners. There were three seedy-looking camels kneeling over by Grim's tent, and three almost as seedy-looking individuals were talking to Grim in the midst of our camp, with most of our gang seated in a semicircle listening. Grim had out his traveling water-pipe for the sake of effect, and was puffing away at it while he meditated on the information that was being drawn forth gradually. Ayisha was seated on the mat beside him.

The man with the squeak in his voice, who did most of the talking, was a very dark-skinned fellow with a short, coal-black, curly beard. He had little gold rings in his ears, and in spite of the filthy condition of his clothes he wore an opulent look--the sort that suggests intimate acquaintance with the fabled riches of the East. I have seen a Moor, who hadn't a coin with which to bless himself, create exactly the same impression by simply being dark and handsome.

He was eating dates while he talked, so I suppose Grim had been to some pains to make him feel welcome. But he hadn't been there long.

"Wallahi!" he said as I joined the circle. "But Your Honor is surely Ali Higg, and that is the lady Ayisha! Your Honor is pleased to pretend otherwise, but am I blind? I, who come straight from Petra where Your Honor paid me, am not thus easily deceived!

"Lo, the good camels! It was easy to make a wide circuit, and reach this place a day ahead of me; but what is Your Honor's purpose? What do you want with me, O Lion of Petra?"

"Nevertheless," said Grim, "I am not Ali Higg, who styles himself Lion of Petra."

"Is that not the lady Ayisha?" he retorted. "True, I have only seen you in the dark, but have I not seen her at the least ten times? Was it not she who had my servant flogged on a former occasion because he likened her to other women?"

Grim said nothing to that. Ayisha drew the embroidered head-cloth over her face, I suppose to hide a smile.

"For what purpose did you visit Petra?" Grim inquired.

"Mashalla! Did I not receive payment from Your Honor? I do not understand!"

"It is I who do not understand," said Grim. "Repeat to me what you did at Petra."

"But Your Honor knows!"

"Very well. Return with me to Petra. I have reasons for asking."

"Wallahi! If it suits Your Honor's humor to make me tell you a tenth time what I have nine times said already, I have a tongue that wags. But I see that another has been telling tales of me behind my back, making me out a liar for his own purposes. *Inshallah,* it shall be found that my tale varies by less than the ten-thousandth part of the width of a hair from what I have told already."

"Proceed," said Grim. "I listen."

"Thus then: While in Jaffa, having received Your Honor's letter by the hand of Shabbas Ali, requesting me to spy on the British troops, I made all haste, laying aside my own affairs and journeying wherever the trail of information led me. I asked questions, but was not content with asking. I went and looked. I made friends with subordinate officials, some of whom I bribed to show me written orders removed from the desks of commanding officers.

"I ascertained all particulars and found this to be the fact: That whereas there are small bodies of troops scattered in certain places, those are needed for local protection of the places where they are; and that whereas there is at Ludd an army of more than twenty thousand men, with guns, great store of supplies, cavalry, and aeroplanes, that army is held in readiness to go to Egypt and cannot for the present be sent against you. Moreover, the long march, so difficult for guns and supply-wagons, from there to Petra, would not be attempted during the hot season. So Your Honor is safe from attack."

"Uh! So you say!" Grim grunted.

You could almost hear the wheels click inside his head as he tried to puzzle out what use to make of this man. One thing was clear enough: the Lion of Petra was well informed. It was nothing less than fact that on no account could an expedition be undertaken against him for a long time. And it was fair, therefore, to presume that in his Petra fastness the robber chief would be feeling confident, and would be that much more difficult to bluff.

But it is one advantage of that land that you may be deliberate without causing impatience or losing respect. Rather the contrary; the Arab values your decisions all the more for being reached after several minutes of silent thought.

Neither our own gang nor the prisoner was in the least disturbed by Grim's taking his time, and only Narayan Singh, still postponing his sleep, was anxious when Ayisha leaned her head close to Grim's and whispered. Grim did not nod or shake his head or make any recognition of her presence--for a real Arab would not have dreamed of doing so--but it was she who gave him the right suggestion, although her intention was totally different from his.

"You lie," he said suddenly.

"Allah!"

"There is an army making ready now to march on Petra."

"As Allah is my witness, there is no such thing."

"You shall return to Petra."

"But Your Honor knows I am in great haste. My own small affairs at Jaffa, God knows, have been neglected. How shall I spare time to return to Petra?"

"And there you shall reverse your story."

"Allah!"

"You shall tell the very numbers and equipment of the army that makes ready."

"May He who never sleeps preserve me! Am I mad, or dreaming? In Petra I have told Your Honor a true tale; shall I return to Petra in order to tell you a lie? O Lord of the limits of the desert, listen to me! I have property in Jaffa; I must attend to it."

"I know you have. By the wharf where the Greeks land melons from Egypt, isn't it? Three godowns and a cafe on the corner? A nice property."

He paused, and I think he was turning over in his mind just how far it would be wise to go with all those others listening; for every word he let fall was sure to be discussed and discussed again at the next halting-place.

"Which is better--to return to Petra and obey, or to lose that property?"

"How shall I lose it? Hah! Your Honor is pleased to joke. You will invade Palestine as far as Jaffa?"

"For those who live under British protection and yet spy against the British are not so well treated by them as those who spy on their behalf."

"Maybe. When they are caught! When they have caught a fox they may skin him."

"And I am not Ali Higg, the Lion of Petra."

"Then who in the name of the Prophet are you, with the Lion's wife at your side?"

"That is none of your business. You come back to Petra with me. No, not your men; they go on. You alone. I have spoken."

In vain the man protested. He did not believe for a moment that Grim was not Ali Higg, and he felt sure that he was being kidnaped for some frightful fate, although Grim's mildness of demeanor must have puzzled him; for according to accounts the real Lion of Petra was a roaring beast.

Grim assigned two men to watch him, and gave the order to strike camp, refusing to listen to any further argument. And since the man's camels were too exhausted to march at once he ordered all three left behind at the oasis and put the prisoner on one of our baggage animals.

Just as we were ready to start he walked over to the two men and threatened them with frightful torture unless they hurried westward the minute the camels were fit to move on. It was pretty obvious that they were only too glad to obey; and Yussuf, our prisoner, made obedience more certain by shouting messages to them to be delivered to friends in Jaffa.

So Narayan Singh cast appraising eyes on the *shibriyah,* and curled up in it like a big dog, without troubling to ask Ayisha's permission. Sleep was his first intention, but he was for killing two birds with one stone; I did not realize at the time what a chance that was going to provide for making the first advances to the lady.

I rode forward beside Grim, who guided us with a compass on his wrist until the stars came out; and for hours on end we went side by side, saying nothing, listening to the monotonous jangle of his camel bell and the obligato of the bells behind. It was music that suited our mood, harmonizing perfectly with the solemn marvel of a desert sunset and the velvety, cool silence of the starlit night.

"That man Yussuf had me guessing," he said at last. "I couldn't place him. Knew his face, but that was all. Then she whispered something about his being a wind that carries smells from one village to the next and back again, spying against both sides at the same time. Then I remembered. He used to spy for us against the Turks and sell them information about us at the same time. Nearly got shot for it, but was let off because his services had really been valuable. I remember his being sent down to Jaffa and told to stay put."

"But what in thunder are you going to do with him?" I asked. "He thinks you're Ali Higg"

Grim chuckled.

"Wonder what Ali Higg will say when he's confronted by Ali Higg!"

"Wonder what he'll do, you mean, don't you!"

"What d'you keep looking back for?"

"Just keeping tabs on Ayisha."

"No need to worry about her. Now we've got Yussuf on our string it's a cinch we can use her whichever way the cat jumps. She'll be afraid he'll tell tales about her."

"Hell!" I said. "It seems to me this whole procession's crazy! The best we've got with us is a gang of professional thieves.

"The farther we go the more we load up with sure-fire traitors. First Ayisha; she'd cut throats at so much per. Her four men, who'd change sides once an hour if they were made afraid that often. Now this Yussuf--a professional spy, whose habit you say is to betray both sides."

"Pretty good outfit, I'll tell the world," he answered.

"Good for what?"

"You got cold feet?"

"I've got cold judgment. We're crazy. We haven't a chance in a million of getting the best of an outlaw with two hundred men."

"We can try, can't we?"

"Yes, and die, can't we!"

"Well--we might do worse. I'd sooner croak in harness than have an eight-horse funeral. But say, if you don't like it you go back and join those two fellows at the oasis. There'll be no hard words."

But I felt too afraid of my own opinion of myself to turn back at that stage of the game.

CHAPTER VIII

"He Cools His Wrath in the Moonlight, Communing with Allah!"

Now the desert at full moon is as light as Broadway, and the only shadows are those the camels cast, than which there is nothing more weird in the whole range of phantasmagoria. We looked like a string of glistening ghosts accompanied by goblins of a fourth dimension mocking us, and though you couldn't see the details of men's faces, looking back along the line you could see every movement and distinguish man from man.

About midnight Ayisha made up her mind to enjoy the *shibriyah,* more, I suspect, for the sake of annoying the Sikh than because she really wanted it. So she ranged alongside, and chiefly because I was curious and chose to be amused, but partly because of my league with Narayan Singh to keep watch on her, I checked my protesting camel and let him drop back into place behind them.

I knew Narayan Singh was awake, for I had seen the glow of his cigarette through the curtains ten minutes before; but he pretended to be asleep, so that she had to get the camels flank to flank and put her hand inside the curtains to awake him. Then he did the obvious thing and seized her hand, and I heard his bass voice answering her shrill protests. I don't know why, but the moonlight that made all things clear seemed also to make words more than usually distinct.

"Ah!" he boomed. "I dreamed of paradise. I awake and find a houri with her hand in mine! Il-hamd'ul-illah![21] I Enter, beloved! Why waste the moonlight hours?"

"Pig!" she retorted. "Father of bristles! Let my hand go!"

"Nay, lovely one! I awake--I see--I understand; thou art not a houri after all, but that same Ayisha I have loved in secret all these burning days! I, who had re-

---

21 Thanks be to God!

solved that gold and honor were as feathers in the scale against thy kisses, am I blessed as last?"

"Cursed by black ifrits, thou son of an Afghan pig! Let me go, and get out of that ***shibriyah!"***

"Such eyes! Behold, the moon is pale beside them, and the stars mere drops of sweat on the sky's dull cheek! Such loveliness as thine, beloved, needs a warrior to worship it--such a man as I, who would cut the throats of kings for a kind word from thee!"

Don't forget, you fellows who have to call on a girl a dozen Sunday evenings in succession before she will go to the movies or condescend to sit out a dance with you, that east of the fifteenth meridian the situation is reversed, and the man who wasn't swift about his wooing would stand no chance at all. Modesty of approach is reckoned a sure sign of unworthiness, and deference as cowardice that fears to seize an opportunity.

"An Indian lover and a boasting louse are one," she answered; but she laughed as she said it, and her voice had lost the shrill note.

"Hah! Try me!" he retorted, tugging at her hand again, and whether or not she tried really hard to release it she failed. "Boasts should be put to the test, beloved! We of the North have a way of understanding our performance. I would burn and lay waste cities for thy sake! Come!"

Her laugh struck a bell-like note now. There was a hint of pleasure in it, and more than a hint of thoughtfulness. You know those overtones of a bell that go fading away into the infinite, in touch, somehow, with thoughts that haven't reached any of us yet except the man who made the bell.

"Ah! Afghans are all alike!"

Sikhs say that of Afghans too, and Afghans say the same thing of the Sikhs.

"You would say anything for me; but as for cutting throats and laying waste, I myself would be the very first victim. Thy love, I think, would burn up and be ashes faster than the cities I should never see."

"Cities! I will take you to all the cities! You shall have your will of the richest! Covet pearls, and I will burn the feet of jewelers until they beg you to take their costliest! Covet rubies, and I will plunder them from the eyes of temple gods! Covet gold, and I will melt down the throne of a maharajah to make bracelets for your ankles!"

"Wallahi! You speak like a braggart."

"Braggart? I? Nay, I am a lover whose words go lamely. They are but chaff blown along the wind of great accomplishment. With thee to fight for I would dare the very rage of Ali Higg!"

He still held her hand. She waited about a minute before answering.

"Which Ali Higg?" she asked at last.

"Any Ali Higg! All Ali Higgs! As lions go down beneath the feet of elephants so shall the Lion of Petra fail before me!"

"One at a time!" she laughed. "There is one Ali Higg who could command you with a word--another who could order your carcass thrown to the vultures. Words first, since your boastings are all words! I say that, for all your brave words, this Ali Higg who rides ahead of us can make you slay me for a word of praise from him."

"You mean, beloved, you could make me slay him for a word of praise from you!" the Sikh lied glibly.

"But I might not want him slain."

"Have him made into a cripple, then--a ruin of a man, for daring to displease you!"

"But he pleases me!"

"Aha! I am jealous! By the beard of the Prophet, Ayisha, beware of my jealousy! I am a man of few words but sudden deeds! Is there a man who stands in my way? May Allah show compassion on him, for he is like to need it!"

He was so fervid in his avowals that he almost convinced me--almost made me believe that his private agreement with me had been a camouflage for his real intentions.

There is precious little of which my friend Narayan Singh isn't capable in the way of romantic soldiering; he ought to have been born two or three hundred years ago as, in fact, according to his reincarnating creed, he was. Perhaps he remembers past lives so vividly that he lives them over again. I wish I could remember a past life or two.

Ayisha was about to answer him when Grim's shrill bosun's whistle that he keeps for emergencies whined from in front, and the sleepy-looking line awoke with a start. Every single rifle down the length of the caravan, including mine, was unslung in a second and the click of the sliding bolts was as businesslike as if we had been a squad on the parade-ground. Narayan Singh, rifle in hand, sprang on to Ayisha's little Bishareen, and she jumped into the *shibriyah,* like a pair doing stunts at the circus.

So far good. But the rest was amateurish. We milled badly. Grim away in front had halted to let the line close, and we swarmed around him like a herd of steers that smell wolves, and nobody seemed to know which way to look, or what to do next.

I was right in the midst of the mess, with a camel on either side trying to get its teeth into me, and what with Grim's shouting to get the tangle straightened, and our all trying to obey at once, it was some minutes before I got the hang of things. In fact, I think I understood last.

We were already surrounded perfectly on three sides by camel-men who kept out of reasonable rifle-range and stalked us like dark ghosts from the rear. They resembled a drag-net, drawing us in the direction of Petra, and the only unblocked segment of the circle was exactly in front of us. Every time I tried to count them there seemed more than before, and there were certainly over a hundred.

I got one close look at Grim's face, and knew he had made his mind up what to do; but all the men were shouting different advice and it was a question whether he would be able to get control before a disaster happened. I said nothing and did nothing but kept fairly close to him. Narayan Singh found his proper place alongside me, with the halter of Ayisha's camel in his hand; and he said nothing either.

Suddenly Grim reached out and seized old Ali Baba by the shoulder, drawing him close and growling into his ear. I could not catch the words, but he repeated them again and again, and Ali Baba nodded vehemently. Not a shot had been fired yet, for Grim had forbidden it, and the other side showed no disposition to do other than surround us at a safe distance. But I noticed they were reducing their estimate of safety and seemed to be gradually closing in for a concerted rush from all sides at once.

Then two things happened suddenly. Out of the open horizon in front, from between two great mounds that looked like ant-heaps, three figures emerged on camels, apparently all alone and unsupported. The one in the middle on the tallest camel made a signal with a long strip of cloth waved like a semaphore against the moonlight.

Instantly the opposing force began to close in, and Ali Baba proved his mettle. Those sons and grandsons obeyed his order as efficiently as he did Grim's. They made a feint all in a cluster together straight for the widest gap in the circle behind us.

The enemy drew off to a safer distance, whereat Ali Baba wheeled and charged another segment of the circle, widening it again. Still not a shot had been fired by either side.

Around Grim now were Narayan Singh, Ayisha, and myself with our prisoner Yussuf, and Ayisha's four. Grim watched his chance and sent me to bring back four of Ali Baba's men, and by the time I had done that he had lessened the distance perceptibly between himself and the three lone individuals in front. He was leaning low over his camel, peering at the three like a seaman staring from a crow's-nest in a fog.

It was a weird business--a swiftly played chess game, almost noiseless; for wherever Ali Baba charged the enemy drew off, while the rest came closer until they were charged in turn.

"It's obvious we're intended to be made prisoners," Grim said to me at last. "But I think it's obvious we're not going to be."

Nevertheless, I understood nothing of his plan, except that our little group kept drawing closer to the three, one of whom seemed in command of the other side. At the moment I suspected that Grim was one of those officers who are splendid at intelligence work and at playing a lone hand, but less than ordinary in the field; Ali Baba looked like the man of action.

Why, with all that brave old man's ability to swing and spur his gang in absolute control, had not the lot of us burst through the circling enemy and made a bolt for it? That was what I should have done.

But suddenly Grim turned and pushed the muzzle of his pistol into Ayisha's face as she leaned out of the *shibrayah* to watch. It caught her under the jawbone, so that she could not see what his finger was doing, and did not dare try to move away.

"Now shout!" he ordered her. "Tell 'em your name *Wallahi!* Yell, or I'll kill you."

She let out a bleat like a frightened goat, that might have been audible thirty yards away if there were no other noise.

"Louder! I'll blow your brains out if you disobey!"

So she screamed at the top of her lungs, making her voice carry as all desert people can. And after she had called three times she was answered by a clear, contralto woman's voice.

"Ay-ish-a! O Ay-ish-a!"

"Jael! Jael!" she called back; and at that the rider of the middle camel waved the cloth again.

As fast as they caught sight of it--in tens and twenties--the oncoming riders halted.

But Ali Baba did not stand still. Neither did we. The three lone individuals in front of us began to approach.

"Come on!" said Grim. "Now's our chance!"

And at last I saw his idea. I did not know which to admire more, the man who had thought of it in that sudden crisis, or Ali Baba who had understood so swiftly and carried out his part so well. But there was no time for admiration then.

All together--Ali Baba and his men along one side of a right-angle and we from the other--we swooped on the three. And there were nine or ten shots fired before we closed on them, though none by our side.

My camel went down under me twenty yards before we reached them. Two other camels were killed, and one of Ali Baba's sons was grazed. But in another second we had captured two men and a woman, and it was too late for the spectators to do anything, unless they cared to risk killing their own leader.

I thrust my way on foot through the milling camels, for I wanted to be in at the death, as it were, and I saw Grim take the woman's rifle away. She looked more surprised than any one I have ever seen--more so than a man I once saw shot in the stomach who looked suddenly into the next world and did not like it.

"Shout to 'em, Jael!" he ordered in plain English. "Call 'em off, or I'll kill you! Shout to 'em; d'you hear!"

"Ayisha! What does this mean? Ali? Ali Higg? You here? I don't understand!"

"You'll be dead before you understand if you don't call those men off," Grim answered; and his pistol demonstrated that he meant it, for her men were closing in on us.

So she knelt up on her camel and cried out that Ali Higg was there, bidding them keep their distance.

"But what does this mean, Ali? And you speak English? Since when? Oh, I must be mad! You are not Ali Higg! No! I see now you are not, but . . ."

She turned on Ayisha and spoke in Arabic: "Ayisha, what does this mean? Answer me!"

But Ayisha said nothing. She chose to get back between the curtains of the **shibriyah,** and I saw Narayan Singh on the far side whispering to her.

"For," as he told me afterward, "the time to persuade a woman you are her friend is when she is afraid or distracted by doubt. At all other times she is like a leopard; but then she is like a lost sheep!"

The silence was at an end now. Every one was shouting; the real Ali Higg's men wanting to know what had happened, and Ali Baba's answering them with threats if they dared disobey and come closer. The effect was exactly as if the figures on a motion-picture screen could be heard calling back and forth.

The two men whom we had captured with the woman Jael were silent, staring hard at Grim as if they saw a vision; and Yussuf, the prisoner we had made at the oasis, tried to talk to them, but they would not listen to him; the drama was too absorbing. Jael herself, inclined to be panicky at first, was recovering self-possession by rapid stages, and grew silent.

She hardly looked like a woman until you came quite close to her, for she was dressed like a man, in the regular Bedouin cloak and head-gear, with a bandolier full of cartridges. But her hair had come unbound, and one long reddish lock of it was over her shoulder.

She had a good-looking, strong face, badly freckled, and was probably about forty years old, although that much was hard guessing in the moonlight; for the rest, she looked like the incarnation of activity--standing still, but only by suppression.

"Now Jael Higg," said Grim, "we'll have no squeamishness about sex. I'm in a tight place, and you'll obey orders or take the consequences. We're going to Petra, the lot of us."

"You! Are coming with me? To Petra?"

"Yes. And we've escort enough. Who commands those men?"

"I!"

"Yes, yes. But who's at the head of them now?"

"Ibrahim ben Ah."

"Call out for Ibrahim ben Ah to come here to speak with Ali Higg, and watch that he comes alone," Grim ordered, and two or three of Ali Baba's men went off to obey. "Now, Jael, you do the talking. Understand me, though; this pistol has a way of going off quite suddenly when the trigger is pressed. Answer: What village were you intending to raid?"

"None."

"No use lying. Ali Higg's spy brought word to him that the British are engaged elsewhere. Raid follows promptly, of course. Now, out with it! I don't need you at Petra; Ayisha will serve my purpose there. You've ten seconds before I pull the trigger. Where was this raid headed for?"

"El-Maan." "Why?"

"That place has become too independent. The tribes meet there and plan raids on their own account."

"Uh-huh. That sounds fairly credible. Now, observe--I pass my pistol to this Indian."

He handed it to me.

"He will shoot you dead if you make one false move. You will tell Ibrahim ben Ah to take all his men at once to that next oasis on the way to El-Maan, and to wait there for yourself and Ali Higg, to wait as long as three days if necessary. Say you will join them there and lead the raid. You understand me?"

"Yes."

"You understand that you will die immediately if you disobey?"

"Yes."

"He will ask what the shooting meant just now. You will answer that there was a mistake owing to the darkness, and that Ali Higg is in a great rage, and he had better make himself scarce. If he asks others questions, curse him and tell him to be off.

"And one last warning, Jael Higg! Obey me exactly, and you shall see your husband in Petra. Disobey by as much as a word or a sign and you're dead. Do we understand each other?"

"You really mean it? You will go to Petra?"

"Yes."

"I have seen fools, and men in love, and gamblers, but you are the greatest mad-man of them all," she answered. "Very well, I will speak to him as you say."

Grim mounted his camel and rode to the top of a ridge of sand about twenty yards away, where he halted and sat motionless. If he really looked so much like Ali Higg, as seemed to be the case, no one at that distance could have doubted his identity. I hauled off two or three paces, so as not to betray the fact that I was to be Jael's executioner in a certain contingency, and the long sleeve of my cloak con-cealed the pistol.

As I am setting down the facts exactly as they happened I may as well record here that I laughed. She thought I laughed at her in cold-blooded delight at the prospect of murder, and I think that tightened her resolution not to give me the least excuse.

But I was not feeling in the least cold-blooded. I was laughing at myself, who might be forced to shoot a woman after all.

Perhaps Grim gave the job to me because he knew I would not shoot her in any case. I don't know. Nor do I myself know now whether I would have shot her; sometimes I think yes, sometimes no. My guess is that I would have failed to do it, and that Narayan Singh, who was standing by and heard every word that passed, would have wiped my eye, as the saying is.

Then Ibrahim ben Ah came striding into our midst like an old-time shepherd with a modern rifle in place of crook, looking neither to the right nor the left of him, but fixing his eyes on the man he thought was Ali Higg on the camel beyond us. He seemed surprised when Jael Higg stopped him, and told him to take all his men at once to that oasis, where he was to wait, if necessary, three days.

"I was told to speak with the Lion himself," he objected. *"Ya sit Jael,*[22] there is wrath for those who disobey him!"

"Go, taste his wrath then!" she retorted. "There was shooting because of a mis-take in the darkness. Good camels were killed. He is more enraged than at the loss of twenty men. He would have it the blame is yours--"

---

22   O lady Jael.

"Mashallah! Mine!"

"But I persuaded him. He cools his wrath in the moonlight, communing with Allah. Better go, Ibrahim, before his mood changes again."

"But how came he to be here ahead of us? We left him in Petra. How--"

"How old beards love to wag! Fool! Go ask him then! I call these men to witness I have given the order that he told me to give to you. I wash my hands!"

She began to make the gesture of washing hands, but thought better of it, for I might have mistaken that for a signal. Old Ibrahim ben Ah looked straight into her eyes, read resolution there, and bowed like a courtier to a queen. Then he turned on his heel, strode back to his camel, mounted, and returned to his men without another word to any one. Yet I dare bet that he had counted us, and knew we were all strangers, and dare say his thoughts would fill a good long chapter of a book.

Grim continued to sit his camel motionless until the raiders under Ibrahim ben Ah had formed into four long lines and ridden away westward, towing enough baggage-animals behind them for a week or two's supplies.

"One hundred and forty men," he announced when they were gone. "The Lion of Petra can't have many left."

CHAPTER IX

"I Think We've Got the Lion of Petra on the Hip!"

G rim is one of those fellows who tell you their principles as grudgingly as they let out facts. He would make the poorest sort of propagandist or politician, for he doesn't advertise, and hates long arguments. What he knows he knows is so because it works; and he proceeds to put it to work.

Nor is he much of a teacher. He takes people as he finds them and adapts his plans accordingly. So it is only from observation extended over a considerable period in all sorts of circumstances that I can say I believe his first and underlying principle is to look for the positive, concrete usefulness in any one with whom he is associated, whether friend or enemy. And this I have heard him say several times.

"In secret service you limit yourself if you make plans. The game is to listen and watch. Presently the other fellow always tells his plans or else betrays them."

And he is no such fool as to be caught in the act of listening, or to forewarn his enemy by seeming to wish to listen.

He gave the order to march at once. Some of the men doubled up uncomfortably on the riding-camels, because of the three that had been killed, and the Bishareen fell to me.

I ranged alongside Jael Higg, with Narayan Singh on the other side of her. At that we were off, Grim leading, well in advance, with Ali Baba and six men in attendance.

The moon was a bit behind us by that time, so that I did not have much chance to observe Jael Higg narrowly until she turned her face to speak to me. But she was not long about doing that--say fifteen minutes--nine hundred seconds; suppressed curiosity can work up a pretty high pressure in that time.

"Who is this man who looks like Ali Higg?" she asked me suddenly, and I had a good look at her face; you don't have to answer questions without thinking, just because they are asked by a woman in a friendly tone of voice.

Her nose was Roman and very narrow, and her dark eyes looked straight at you without their pupils converging, which produced a sensation of being seen through. She had splendid teeth; and her mouth, which was humorous, turning upward at the corners when she smiled, had nevertheless a certain suggestion of stealthy strength--perhaps cruelty. Her chin was firm and practical. So were her freckled hands. I decided that the less I said the better.

"He is a sheikh," said I pretty abruptly.

She turned that empty information over in her mind for a minute, and decided to turn her guns on me. Conversation was not easy, for we were swinging along at a great pace, and my camel was a lot smaller than hers.

"And you are an Indian? How is it that you speak English?"

"Many of us speak it. We pass our college examinations in English."

"How do you come to be with that--that sheikh?" she asked next.

"It pleases me to follow him. *Inshallah,* I may help him in case of sickness."

"You are a *hakim?*"

I admitted that, although secretly pitying any poor devil who might pin faith to the claim.

"Ali Higg--the real one, who is known as the Lion of Petra--believes in Indian *hakims,* like all these Arabs who have no use for European doctors. And this big man on my left, who is he?"

"My servant."

"An Afghan?"

"A Pathan."

She turned that over in her mind, too, for several minutes.

"And how does Ayisha come to be with you?" she asked at last.

At that Narayan Singh broke silence, and although he denied it afterward I know that his only motive was to get a little preliminary vengeance on Ayisha for the names she had called him. He maintains that he was "casting a stone, as it were, into a pond to see which way the ripples went."

"Few women will refuse to follow a Pathan when honored by his admiration," he boomed.

I could not see her face then, because she was staring at Narayan Singh.

"Do you realize whose wife you are tampering with?" she asked him.

"Hah! Where I come from a man must guard his women if he hopes to keep them."

"Where you are going to, such a man as you will find his own life hard enough to keep," she retorted.

"*Bismillah!* I have kept it thus far," said Narayan Singh.

She turned to me again.

"What does the sheikh of yours call himself?"

"Hajji Jimgrim bin Yazid of El-Abdeh."

"Jimgrim. Jimgrim. Where have I heard that name?"

"The stars have heard it," roared Narayan Singh loud enough for the stars to hear him boast. "He has taken the Lion of Petra's shape. He has taken his name. He has taken his wife. And now he will take his den. *Akbar,* Jimgrim Ali Higg of Petra!"

Mahommed the poet was riding two or three behind us in the line, and heard that. He took the cue and began his song. In a minute the whole line was roaring the refrain, and it broke like volleys on the night:

"*Akbar! Akbar! Jimgrirn Ali Higg!*"

Jael Higg laughed. "He has a fool's luck and a lusty band of followers," she said. "It was only because Ayisha called out that he caught me. But a fool's luck is like a breath of wind that passes--"

Suddenly she sat bolt upright and raised her right hand.

"Oh, this night! This madness! Of all the dreams, of all the hallucinations, this is the wildest! I warned Ali Higg! I told him my foreboding, and he laughed!"

She looked down at me again, and studied me for half a minute.

"Tell me," she went on, "is that Sheikh Jimgrim of yours mad, or am I mad?"

"If you ask my opinion, as a *hakim,*" I answered, "you were mad to sit your camel alone, with only two men, within reach of our Jimgrim."

"What does he think he will do with me at Petra?"

"He thinks silently," said I.

Whereat she too was silent for a few minutes, and then broke out into a new tirade of exclamations, but this time in a language of which I knew not one word--perhaps Russian, or Slovak, or Bulgarian. I think she was praying in a sort of wild way to long-neglected saints.

She gave me the impression of being mentally almost unhinged by the sudden anticlimax of helplessness after over-confidence. Yet when she spoke again her voice was calm, and not without a ring of rather gallant humor.

"I suppose he thinks he has stolen the queen bee, and so has the swarm in his power. But the swarm can sting, and will come for the queen bee."

"So they bring their honey with them, who minds that?" Narayan Singh retorted.

He was enjoying himself, acting the part of a bandit's follower with perfect gusto.

"Oh, so it is honey you are after? And you two are Indians--a Pathan and--"

"From Lahore," said I.

"Five thousand pounds would buy your services?"

"Five thousand promises would make us laugh," said the Sikh.

"How much will your sheikh ever pay you? In an hour I will show you a *wady* down which we three can escape. Agree to that and you shall have five thousand each the same hour that we reach Petra."

"*Wallahi!* Doubtless!" laughed Narayan Singh. "Five thousand bastinados each from Ali Higg, while the queen bee laughs at us for fools! Nay, lady Jael, you are Jimgrim's prisoner."

"Jimgrim!" she said. "Somewhere I have heard that name."

And she turned it over in her mind again like a taster trying wine, not speaking again for nearly an hour, until we drew abreast of a chaos of irregular great boulders that partly concealed the mouth of a gorge as dark and ugly as the throat of Tophet.

"There is your chance!" she said. "Will you take it? You shall have employment with the Lion of Petra! Come!"

But neither of us answered, and I kept a bright lookout for a pistol she still might have concealed on her; for she had not been searched--there was none who could do that with decency except Ayisha, who was not to be trusted.

I knew Grim would not halt again before morning because the camels would not feed properly until after daylight, even if you put corn in front of them. We were likely in for a forced march on Petra, and he would not choose to halt twice if it could be helped. And I supposed that when we did halt he would look to Narayan Singh and me for information.

Yet Mrs. Ali Higg number one was hardly a person you could expect to answer questions truthfully; and even until the stars began to grow pale in the east ahead of us I possessed my soul in patience.

Then: "Is it money your Sheikh Jimgrim wants?" she asked at last. "Does he hold me to ransom? If so, I will give him a draft on the Bank of Egypt. I have Ali Higg's seal here, and I write all his letters."

I did not answer, but Narayan Singh checked his camel a stride or two to make a signal to me behind her back.

"Hah!" he remarked with an air of triumph. And I took that to mean that in his judgment Jimgrim could find use for Ali Higg's seal.

But of course she heard him, and she took it to mean that she had guessed rightly. She turned to Narayan Singh; and because in that land, as an almost invariable rule, no business with a chief can be accomplished without bribing his minions, she worked off a little spite and offered largesse with the same hand.

"Arrange good terms for me and you shall have Ayisha."

"But I have her," said Narayan Singh with a great laugh.

"Maybe. But you haven't settled yet with Ali Higg. Arrange good terms for my ransom, and I will see that Ali Higg wipes off Ayisha's score."

"We shall see about that; we shall see," he answered.

"Yes, yes! You go and see! Go to him now!"

"When we halt," the Sikh answered.

"In an hour it may be too late," she insisted. "If Ali Higg is prowling and should swoop down on you who would bargain then?"

By that time it was light enough to see clearly at close range, and Narayan Singh caught my eye behind her back. I nodded. If there were any likelihood of Ali Higg being on the prowl why should she be in such a hurry to make terms?

Right then Grim called a halt--none too soon for the camels--in a semicircular space protected by a low cliff that might have been a quarry-face two thousand years ago; what might have been a pit was all filled in by drifted sand. But he had his own mat spread on the top of the cliff, whence he could keep an eye on the surrounding country, and gave none of the prisoners a chance to talk to him.

Nobody helped Jael Higg from her camel, for she jumped down like an acrobat and stood staring about her at Ali Baba's gang, and being stared at as they went about the business of off-loading the complaining beasts. I saw Ayisha get out of the *shibriyah,* face around slowly, and meet Jael's eyes.

Neither woman spoke for a minute, or made any sign, but you could almost see the alternating current of scorn and hate that passed between them. Then Ayisha fell back on insolence and walked past Jael deliberately, with dark eyes flashing and a thin smile on her lips.

"So you are now a Pathan's light o' love?" Jael sneered in Arabic.

At that Ayisha turned again and faced her.

"Who speaks? She whom the Lion could not trust to go to Hebron? ***Um Kulsum!***" [23]

Ayisha passed on with a scornful shoulder movement. Narayan Singh grinned with malicious amusement. And I was just in time to catch two of the men again attacking my medicine-chest. Instead of trying to open it they were dragging it along the ground, and they were as pleased with themselves as two small dogs caught burying a boot.

"She has given us money!"

"Who has?"

"The lady Ayisha. We are to bring her this, and she will take poison from it and put it in the other woman's food! So Jimgrim will be rid of her, and all will be well!"

I got Narayan Singh to keep his eye on the chest, and walked up to where Grim was going through the form of Moslem prayer, facing Mecca on his mat on the low hilltop. That was for the benefit of the prisoners, no doubt.

To save time I got down on my knees beside him and went through the same motions, keeping a bright lookout for interruptions and telling him in low tones all that had taken place, repeating conversations word for word as well as I could recall them.

---

23 Um Kulsum was a lady in Arabic legend whose immoralities have made her name a byword.

At last we both squatted, facing each other, and he lighted a cigarette; but it was several minutes yet before he answered.

"Wants to make terms in a hurry, eh? And has the Lion's seal with her?" he said at last.

"Well, as old Ali Baba keeps repeating, Allah makes all things easy! It's a little soon to talk yet, but I think we've got the Lion of Petra on the hip!"

CHAPTER X

"There's No Room for the Two of You!"

Of course, no committee in the world ever yet did more than cloud an issue with argument. It takes one man to lead the way through any set of circumstances, and the only wise course for a committee is to make that man's decision unanimous and back it loyally. But men have their rights, as Grim is always the first to admit.

Ali Baba came and joined us on the cliff-top, and Narayan Singh was not long following suit. The Sikh said nothing, but Ali Baba was conscious of the weight that years should give to his opinion, as well as justly proud of his night's work, and not at all disposed to sit in silence.

"Now the right course, Jimgrim, is to make a great circuit and carry these two women back across the British border," he began at once. "The Lion of Petra will then pay us all large sums of money, without which you will refuse to intercede with the government on his behalf for their return. Thus every one will be satisfied except the Lion, who will be too poor for a long time afterward to have much authority in these parts. Moreover, it will be told for a joke against him, and he will lose in prestige. I am an old man, who knows all about these matters."

"What do you think, Narayan Singh?" Grim asked.

"Sahib, what are we but a flying column? Swiftness and surprise are our two advantages. We should be like a javelin thrown from ambush that seeks out the enemy's heart. If we fail we are but a lost javelin--an officer, a sepoy, a civilian and a handful of thieves--there are plenty more! If we succeed there is a deed done well and cheaply! I never hunted lions, but I have seen a tiger trapped and beaten. Have we not good bait with us?"

There followed a hot argument between Arab and Sikh, each accusing the other of ulterior motives as well as ignorance and cowardice; in fact, they acted like any other committee, growing less and less parliamentary as their views diverged. Ali Baba seemed to consider it relevant to call Narayan Singh a drunkard, and the Sikh considered it his duty in the circumstances to refer to Ali Baba's jail record. In the midst of all that effort to solve the problem at Petra, Grim asked me to go and invite Jael Higg to join us.

In that hard, uncharitable desert daylight she did not impress me very favorably. The lines of her freckled face suggested too much ruthlessness, as though she was positively handsome in a certain way--as long as you observed the whole effect and did not study details--there was a look of cold experience about her brown eyes that chilled you. Of course, she was tired and that made a difference; but I did not find it easy to feel sympathetic, and I thought she was hardly the woman to win a jury's verdict on the strength of personal appeal.

Nevertheless, with all the odds against her, she accomplished that morning what I had never done, or seen done, although many have attempted it and failed. She contrived to tear away Grim's mask and to expose the man's real feelings.

He was always an enigma to me until that interview, at which they squatted facing each other on Grim's mat, with me beside Grim and the Sikh and Ali Baba glaring daggers at each other on either hand. The early sun seemed to edge everybody with a sort of aura, but it also showed every detail of a face and made it next to impossible to hide emotion.

She opened the ball. I imagine she had been doing that most of her life.

"Jimgrim," she said. "Jimgrim. Are you by any chance the American named James Grim, who fought with Lawrence in Allenby's campaign?"

Grim astonished us all by admitting it at once. The name Jimgrim sounds enough like Arabic to pass muster; and we wondered why he should have gone to all that trouble to disguise himself, only to confess his real name when there seemed no need. Even Ali Baba left off cursing the Sikh under his breath.

"I am glad to know that," she said. "It will save my wasting words. No man could ever get your reputation without being ruthless. I won't annoy you by pleading for mercy."

And she looked at once as merciless as she expected him to be.

"Now, Jael Higg," he answered, "let's talk sense."

"You're a rare one, if you can!" she retorted.

"Let's do our best," he said kindly.

She looked very keenly at him for thirty seconds, and seemed to make up her mind that she had no chance against him.

"Very well," she said. "I'll begin by being sensible. How much money do you want?"

It is true that the more you analyze Grim's face the more he does impress you as a keen business man. But there are modifying symptoms. He did not appear to have heard the question.

"I want you to be straightforward and tell me all you know of Ali Higg's circumstances."

"Yes. I'd expect you to want that. As an American hired by the British to help them exploit this country, that's what you would ask. After you know all about him you can fix the ransom. That right? Well, I won't tell."

"I hoped we were going to talk sense," he answered quietly.

"How can any one talk sense with a man like you? What are you doing in this country? `Horning in' is what they'd call it in America. You've got no business here. It's different in my case. I'm married to Ali Higg. I've thrown in my lot with these people. I've a right to help them to independence. But what right have you got to interfere? Bah! Name your price. I'll pay if I can."

"Well, Jael," he answered with a rather whimsical smile. "I'll try to disillusion you to begin with. Perhaps if you understand me better you'll be reasonable.

"All I know is Arabic and Arabs. I've no other gifts, and I like to be some use in the world. I'm real fond of Arabs. It 'ud tickle me to see them make good. But I can see as far through a stone wall as any blind horse can, and I know--better maybe than you do, Jael--that all they'll get by cutting loose and playing pirates is the worst end of it. I hate to see them lose out, so I use what gifts I've got in their behalf."

"Do you call it helping us to come out against Ali Higg and kidnap his wives?" she retorted. "Ali Higg is a patriot. He's against all foreign control of Arab country, and he's man enough to fight.

"These British and French and Italians promised us an independent Arab country. Where is it? Have you seen any of it? No. And you're helping the British break their promise!

"Ali Higg is doing his best to redeem what Arabs fought for in the war, and I'm his wife. You ask me to betray him? Never!"

"Ali Higg is doing his worst, not his best, Jael."

"He is creating unity among these tribes," she retorted.

"He is practically forcing the British to come out and smash him," said Grim. "Now, see here, Jael, I don't want him smashed. I don't hold with his method, but that's the Arab's business; if being crucified and shot for differences of opinion suits them, why, no doubt Ali Higg's the right man for them. They tell me he delivers the goods. But he can't go starting a new war out here, not while I've any say he can't."

"Who are you that should say or not say?" she demanded.

"Same as Ali Higg, Jael; I'm a human. He's from Arabia, you're from the Balkans, I'm from the U.S. We're all three foreigners, aren't we?"

"Yes. But he and I are foreigners who will drive the British out--"

"And let French or Italians in."

"Ali Higg is a fighter, I tell you! He's an Arab, and he knows how to control Arabs just as the Prophet Mohammed did. He has only begun in a small way, but--"

"But he'll wind up like a small-town sport in the lock-up, the way he's going," said Grim. "Now, see here, Jael, I'm just as set on doing my bit in the world as Ali Higg is. Maybe I'm a mite more tolerant, but there isn't a man or woman living who can shift me off a course once I'm set on it.

"Ali Higg considers the Arabs need a holy war. I'm hell bent for peace. I'm going to stop him. I'm not arguing that point, for it won't bear arguing, and I'm not trying to convert you. But you're in my power, and though I sure would hate to inconvenience a lady, I'm that plumb remorseless I'd separate you from Ali Higg for ever unless you helped me call him off the warpath."

"Help you!" she exclaimed with horror.

"Sure. You've got to! There's no law this side of the border, Jael, that can make me hand you over to authority. There's no mandate out here yet. There never will be one if I can prevent it. I'm here to keep a foreign army from trespassing across the Jordan, it being my crazy notion that Arabs can evolve their own government, if let. You've got to help me keep that foreign army out, or take the consequences."

She laughed at last. It was rather a hard laugh without much mirth in it.

"Your words are a liar's, but your voice rings true," she said. "I think you're only another of these diplomatists."

"I'm that diplomatic I'm chancing my hide to save other peoples," he answered. "Let's be quite frank, Jael. I'm in danger out here. All I've got with me besides two respectable men are thieves from El-Kalil. That little army of Ali Higg's lies between me and the border, and I'm no kind of a darn-fool optimist when it comes to figuring on Ali Higg's hospitality in Petra. Nor am I kidding myself I can persuade His Dibs by a theological argument or any cheap advice.

"But I've reasoned it out this way--if Ali Higg sends Ayisha to El-Kalil rather than trust you to do your shopping, that's because he sets a value on you. Since he sends you out in charge of a raid on El-Maan I guess he sets a high value on you. That's as good as saying you've got influence. Believe me, Jael, you'll use that influence to suit my plans or we're not going to be friends!"

"Friends?" she said, and stared at him.

"Sure. Why not? Look at the men I've got with me; they're all my friends. I'm right proud to say it. I might have hanged most of them once, but I never knew it do much good to a man to hang him; so we get acquainted, and one way and another we contrive to keep on good terms.

"See my point? Nobody'd hang you if I scooted back over the border with you, Jael. There isn't a law that would cover your case. But they'd deport you, and you'd be an outcast with tabs kept on you, and I've seen your sort come to a bad end. I never liked to see it. I never saw anybody gain by it. I'd sooner see you winning every one's respect by sticking to Ali Higg and schooling him to play safe."

Her pale face actually blushed under the freckles. She had not lived in America for nothing. As the wife of a polygamist she knew exactly what he meant about winning respect. Her sort enjoys to be patronized by reformers and social uplifters about as much as an eagle likes a cage.

"You talk well," she said, "but you must be a fool at bottom, or you wouldn't suggest friendship with me. Can you imagine me not pushing you into Ali Higg's clutches at the first chance?"

"Sure I can, or I wouldn't waste time talking. You've got more sense than that,

Jael. You might trick me. It has been done. Ali Higg might scupper me and the crowd--he mighty likely would. But that 'ud be the end of Ali Higg's prospects, for as sure as my name's Grim the British would smash him to avenge me, and you know it! If they didn't get you they'd get him, and you'd become the property of the first petty chief who could lay his hands on you. So let's talk like two sensible people."

"You'll find me sensible," she answered. "I shall just do nothing--tell you nothing."

"You've told too much already to be able to stop now, Jael," he answered, smiling. "I'm sure you won't put me to the necessity of searching you; you've too much pride for that. So suppose you pass me Ali Higg's seal--the one you sign all his letters with. No, don't try to hide it in the sand; put it here."

He held his hand out, and she bit her lip in mortification. It was too bad that she had made that slip of boasting to Narayan Singh and me about the seal, but there was nothing else for it now and she gave it to him--a gold thing as big as a silver half-dollar, marvelously engraved.

"That settles the financial end of it," said Grim. "We can impound all that money in the Bank of Egypt--although I'm free to admit I wouldn't take such a seal away from a friend of mine."

"Give it back, then," she answered with a bitter little laugh. "I see I'll have to be your friend."

He smiled--wonderfully gently. There wasn't the least offense in it, although there wasn't any credulity either.

"I always aim to prove myself a man's friend--or a woman's," he said, "before expecting to be trusted out of sight. I dare say that's your code too?"

"If ever Ali Higg catches you with that seal--"

"He won't catch me, Jael; he won't catch me. But you shall have it back, and the money shan't be touched, if you play straight."

She shrugged her shoulders petulantly, admitting defeat but resenting it. There came a time, months later, when she understood Grim's peculiar altruism and respected it, but she was a long way just then from admiring him.

"You force me," she said. "Name your terms."

"Well, then, suppose we speak of Ali Higg to begin with. Is his temper uneven?

Is there any way to catch him in a specially good humor?"

"He's the most even-tempered man I know," she laughed. "He's always in a rage."

"So much the easier for us," Grim answered. "That kind always make mistakes. He must have counted on your brains exclusively to keep him on top; and now your brains are in my pocket, so to speak. How's his health? Boils? Indigestion?"

She nodded.

"Ah! Most angry men have indigestion. Dislikes European doctors, I dare say? Thought so; most fanatical Moslems do that. But an Indian *hakim?* Now, many an Indian *hakim* knows how to relieve indigestion--in between the bouts of rage. D'you suppose he'd entertain a *hakim?*"

She nodded again.

"Well, we'll fix it so a *hakim* can relieve his boils and indigestion. But let you and me understand each other first, Jael. I can be a mean man when I must, but I'll always take a heap of trouble to find a white man's way of accomplishing the same purpose. I can act mean toward you--sheer plug-ugly if you force my hand--but I'd sooner not; and I'd just as lief help you as hinder you, provided you don't upset what I'm seeking to build."

She laughed again, and not so bitterly.

"You're on the wrong side of the wall to build much," she answered. "You should come over into our camp. You're so like Ali Higg in certain lights and in some of your gestures, and so unlike him in other things, that if you came across the Jordan for good I think you could show us something."

Her eyes said far more than her lips did. She was studying him from a new angle--a thoughtful, speculative angle that vaguely excited her.

"What I mean is just this," he said; "that you and I had better decide to be real friends, and not half-open enemies, each looking for a chance to spoil the other's game. There are men in this camp who'll tell you that I keep my word. I'm willing to pledge it not to hurt you or Ali Higg, provided you pledge yours to be equally friendly and to help me in taming Ali Higg so's he'll be useful and not just an ordinary trouble-maker."

"Would you accept my word?" she asked him--ready to consider him fool or liar, according to how he answered.

"I'll accept it, Jael. Sure. For you'll have to give it, and it's all you've got to trade with. And I'll watch you just about twice as carefully as examiners watch the bank directors of New York State.

"Knowing you're watched, like them you're going to be too proud to cheat; and after you've found how it pays to play straight with me you're going almost to enjoy being watched for the sake of the advertisement."

Her face did not soften in the least; but it changed expression, like a woman buyer's who has decided to make a purchase but has not done bargaining.

"I think I'm going to like you," she said. "Of course, you're a liar, like all men, but you've a finer touch than most."

At that point Ali Baba made his first contribution to the argument. The old man did not know much English, but there are certain words--such as liar, cheat, swine, thief, and the list of oaths--that find their way like water to the common level and are known from Spitzbergen to the Horn.

"He is no liar!" he exclaimed in Arabic. "A cunning man with the brain of three, who can use the truth for his own ends! A keeper of secrets! An upsetter of plans! But he is no liar, and I will not hear him called one by a woman! Peace, thou fool! It is written that a woman's tongue is worse than water dripping through a roof!"

It is manners in that country to sit silent while an old man speaks, and even Jael Higg did not offer to rebuke him for the interruption. When he had quite finished Grim took up the argument again.

"Now let's know where we stand. Are you and I to be friends, Jael?"

She nodded.

"I'm no half-way adventurer. I'll make your fortune," she said, "if you'll come the whole way with me, and stay this side of Jordan."

He shook his head and smiled back at her.

"You've your work cut out to keep Ali Higg off the rocks, Jael."

"There's no room for two of you," she answered darkly.

"I guess not."

She looked hard at me, and back from me to Grim. I don't know yet whether she was setting a trap for us or really in earnest about what she said next. Grim thinks she was drawing a bow at a venture.

"Is this the *hakim?* One of the two respectable persons you have with you?

Hm! Respectability is a mask--often a safe mask, often an offensive one, always a lie. All really dangerous criminals are respectable people.

"And a *hakim,* eh? An Indian physician? I have heard of Indian physicians being poisoners--although, of course, they're respectable people and give the poison by mistake! Now if he should go to Ali Higg and poison him, while pretending to cure boils and indigestion--"

"But he won't," said Grim, "so why suppose?"

"Of course he won't, unless you tell him to!" she snapped.

"I dare say he's as much in your power as I am. But suppose you tell him to--"

"I won't, Jael."

"Now don't you be a fool, James Grim! You can't deceive me into thinking you're above such things. That haughty attitude is British, not American; you've been defiled by contact with them. Come out into the open like an unhypocritical American. Talk business.

"I've tried to make a man of Ali Higg, but he's only an animal after all. The best I can ever do with him will be failure compared to what I could make of you, James Grim. You look enough like him to make it possible to substitute you with care. Go ahead and send your *hakim.*"

Grim smiled with perfect good humor, but a blind man could not have mistaken his refusal.

"Oh, you're all hypocrites, you men--Americans, English, French--you're all alike; glad to see a man die, if he's a nuisance, but afraid to admit you'd a hand in it. But you needn't fear. You can send your *hakim* uninstructed. He's an Indian, isn't he? Well, Ali Higg is sure to insult him to the very marrow of his bones, and you can safely leave Indian revengefulness to do the rest."

Grim shook his head.

"He'd be too afraid he might meet me some day. He knows I'd not stand for it. No, Jael; I invited you to talk sense. You've got to make shift with Ali Higg `as is'. If you don't like it say so now and I'll tell off three or four of my thieves to escort you over the border into British territory while I play this game without you.

"What you've got to understand first and last is that I'm dead set on clipping Ali Higg's claws. I don't care a row of imitation pewter shucks about any man's ambition, or any woman's past. My job in the world is to do what I'm able to do, and I'm going to prevent war in this land if I get killed doing it and have to ruin you in the bargain! Now, are we set?"

"I think you're a fool," she said, "and you think me a villain. We're strange partners! Very well, let's try."

Promptly he handed her an envelop, sheet of paper, and his fountain-pen.

"Write first, then, to Ibrahim ben Ah. He knows your hand, I suppose? Tell him there is news of a British force coming over the border, and that he must stay at that oasis in readiness to attack after Ali Higg has taken steps to draw the British in the right direction.

"Say he may have to stay there a week or ten days, and that he is to enforce the death penalty on any of his men who dares try to leave the oasis. Tell him that secrecy as to his present whereabouts is the all-important point. For that reason strangers may be made prisoner and held until further orders. The messenger who bears this is to be sent back with an answer immediately."

"How much of that is true about a British force?" she demanded. "Are you trying to trap those men?"

"None of it's true. No, they're safe. You write, and I'll sign it with your seal."

She hesitated, but I don't know whether from caution or from a genuine dislike to deceive her husband's loyal henchman. But there was no way of getting out of it except by blunt refusal, involving the threatened escort into British territory and deportation. So she wrote, and Grim sealed the letter: He handed it to Ali Baba.

"Select the most trustworthy of your sons, O King of Thieves, give him the fastest camel, and let him ride with that to the oasis. Bid him ride hard and overtake us with the answer."

"Do you think my sons have wings?" asked Ali Baba.

"Not unless devils are winged!" laughed Grim. "It is a simple matter--just there and back again."

"Not so simple, Jimgrim! It is written that in the desert all men are enemies. What if he should meet a dozen men?"

"The letter will be his pass. He must take a chance returning."

"Wallahi! A letter? A pass into Jehannum possibly! By Allah, Jimgrim, a man needs more than a letter in these parts. He needs brains--age--influence--experience. Nay! If any is to take that letter, let me do it. I am old, and they hesitate to kill

an old man. I am wise in the desert ways, not rash. And if they do kill me, then it is only an old man's body bloating in the sun.

"Besides, I am cunning and can give wise answers, whereas those sons of mine might take offense at an insult, or recognize a blood enemy at the wrong moment. Nay, it is I who must take that letter."

Grim clapped him on the back.

"Good, my father; you shall go. Take one son with you to look after your comforts."

He turned that suggestion over in his mind for several minutes, but shook his head finally.

"I go alone. They would ask me why two men bring one letter. Moreover, they might send the one back with an answer, retaining the other as hostage; for it is the way of the devil to put suspicion in men's minds. Two men would double their doubt, just as two stones weigh the twice of one. And I will not take the best camel, but the worst one."

"Why?"

"Write me a second letter. Have the woman write it, and you affix the seal. Give order that they are to provide a swift, fresh camel in exchange for my weary beast. I shall make a great fuss about the beast they provide, rejecting this and that one, thus causing them to believe in me, since men without proper authority do not act thus, but are content with anything so be they can only escape unharmed."

So the second letter was written; and in the rising, scorching heat old Ali Baba set off, mounted on the meanest of the baggage beasts, whose hump was getting galled, so that he wasn't likely to be of much use to us within a day or so.

Then we all got under the shelter of the low tents to give the other camels a rest and wait for evening, and I think Jael Higg slept, but I don't know, for we gave her a tent to herself; she refused point blank to share one with Ayisha.

And Ayisha, I know, did not sleep. She came in the noon glare to the tent I occupied with Narayan Singh and entered without ceremony, slipping through the low opening with the silent ease that comes naturally to the Badawi. She squatted down in front of us, and I awoke the Sikh, who was snoring a chorus from Wagner's "Niebelungen Ring."

For a moment I thought he was going to resume the night's flirtation, but there was something in the quiet manner of her and the serious expression of her face that he recognized as quickly as I did. All her imperious attitude was gone. She did not look exactly pleading, nor yet cunning; perhaps it was a blend of both that gave her the soft charm she had come deliberately armed with.

Of this one thing I am absolutely sure; whatever that young woman did was calculated and deliberate; and the more she seemed to act on impulse the more she had really studied out her move.

Narayan Singh checked a word half-way, and we waited for her to speak first. Her eyes sought mine, and then the medicine-chest. Then she looked back at me, and I made a gesture inviting her to speak.

"You told me," she said at last, "that you have poison in that box that would reach down to hell and slay the ifrits. Give me some of it."

"*Ya sit Ayisha.* I need it all for the ifrits," I answered.

"I will make no trouble for you," she said; and for a moment I suspected she meant to kill herself.

"You are young and beautiful," I told her. "The world holds plenty of good for you yet."

At that she flashed her white teeth and her eyes blazed.

"Truly! Allah puts a good omen into your mouth, *miyan!*[24] Yet little comes to the woman who neglects to plan for it. Give me the poison. I will pay."

I was about to refuse abruptly, being rather old-maidish about some things and not always ready with a smile for what I don't approve; but Narayan Singh interrupted in time to prevent the unforgivable offense of preaching my own code of morals uninvited.

"Tell us who is to be poisoned," he demanded.

"That is none of your business," she answered calmly.

"But the poison is our business," said the Sikh. "We make terms. If the person to be poisoned is an enemy of ours, well and good; you shall have it and we shall be gainers. But Allah forbid that we should hasten the death of a friend! Is it for Jael Higg?"

"No, for I see that to poison her would be to incur the enmity of Jimgrim. Already he takes counsel with her; did he and she not lay their heads together in your

---

24 *Miyan:* the rather contemptuous form of address that Arabs use toward Indian Moslems

presence after morning prayers?"

"For whom, then? For Jimgrim?"

"God forbid! Shall I woo a dead man? Nay! You say you will give me the poison if I tell? You swear it? Then it is for the Lion of Petra. Thus I shall win the love of Jimgrim. And Jael, being without a man, will run away to Egypt, where her money is."

"Bismillah!" swore the Sikh. "I see no reason why I should not get an angry husband out of the way so simply! But remember, Ayisha, you must slay me in turn if you hope to have Jimgrim for husband. By my beard and the Prophet's feet[25] it is I who will have you to wife, if I have to burn kingdoms first!"

"Give me the poison first, and we shall see," she laughed.

"Very well; leave us for a while, Ayisha. I will persuade this master of mine, who has a vein of caution, since he lacks the zeal of love. I will bring you the stuff when he and I have talked it over."

"Strong, strong stuff," she insisted. "Stuff that would eat iron. Ali Higg's belly is tough."

"It shall come out through his flesh like flame," the Sikh promised.

As soon as she had gone, and he had watched her out of earshot, he turned to me with a gruff laugh.

"Now, sahib, make her up a potion of some harmless powder for me to carry to her tent while you go and tell our Jimgrim what has passed. Give her physic that will purge the Lion of Petra without doing worse than make his belly burn. Stay; give croton in a bottle; that is best."

---

25   A scandalous piece of blasphemy

CHAPTER XI

"That We Make a Profit from this Venture!"

Late that afternoon, before they loaded up the camels, there was another conference between Grim, Jael Higg, Narayan Singh, our prisoner Yussuf, and myself. The ancient hills of Edom were not far away, and we were near enough to Petra to feel nervous. Jael made a pretty good pretense of meeting Grim half-way, and I think she had made up her mind to let him dig his own pit and tumble into it.

Yussuf was aware by that time, if not of Grim's identity, at any rate of the fact that he was an officer in the British pay, and was rather obviously considering which would likely pay him best--to side secretly with Ali Higg or openly with Grim, or both.

Having fought over all that country under Lawrence, and knowing consequently every yard of it, I suppose Grim felt neither thrilled nor mystified; but in case any scientist reads this and wants to know how I felt, "fed up and far from home" about describes it. But there was worse to come!

Grim turned to me at last and smiled in that darned genial way he has when he means to call on your uttermost patience or endurance.

"You see, the difficulty is," he said, "to get to Ali Higg without his getting us first. He has probably got between forty and fifty men in Petra with him, so we daren't invade the place. Yet we've got to hurry, because old Ibrahim ben Ah with that army may get suspicious and send back a messenger on his own account. Now, do you feel willing to beard the Lion in his den?"

"Alone?" I asked.

I never felt less willing to do anything, and dare say my face betrayed it.

"No. Narayan Singh will go too, and, of course, Ayisha."

Ayisha seemed about as safe an ambassador to send as an electric spark to a barrel of powder. I glanced at Narayan Singh and felt ashamed, for his eyes glowed unmistakably. He was enthusiastic.

Well, it seems I draw a color-line after all. I can't fight like a Sikh, or be as good a man in lots of ways; but I'm not going to be outdone by one in daring, while the Sikh is looking.

"All right," I said, "I'll do anything you say."

But I did not have the perfect voice-control I would have liked, and Jael Higg grinned. That naturally settled it.

"Narayan Singh needn't come if he'd rather stay with you," I added, and the Sikh raised his eyebrows.

"Do you dare to make love to Ayisha, sahib?" he grinned.

I began to see the general drift of the plan of campaign, and wondered. Having seen more than a little of the Near East, and knowing how the peace of the whole world depends on preserving that unmelted hotpot of nations from anarchy, I was not impressed by the stability of things in general!

Grim had come out on his hair-raising venture because no army was available to deal with Ali Higg, and he would not have ventured unless powers-that-pretend-to-be were sure that Ali Higg was deadly dangerous. Did the peace of the world, then, depend on the success or otherwise of a Sikh's mock love-making. It did look like it.

Narayan Singh got to his feet with a laugh and a yawn, and went to dance attendance on Ayisha, while Grim reinstructed Yussuf regarding the ease with which the British could impound his Jaffa property; but though I listened to all that, and heard Yussuf's vows of fidelity--heard him promise to reverse his former report and spread rumors in Ali's camp of a British army getting ready to advance--the prospect to me looked gloomier and gloomier.

"You can only die once," Grim laughed after a quick glance at my face, "and we may save a hundred thousand people from the sword."

But I suppose I wasn't cut out to be a willing martyr. It was a case of making a silk purse out of a sow's ear, and though I did go forward on that mad escapade it was fear that drove me--fear of the Sikh's and Grim's contempt, and of my own self-loathing afterward.

Grim and Narayan Singh are made of the real hero stuff. I wonder how many others there are like me, who face the music simply because one or two others have got guts enough to lead us up to it.

We didn't move far that night, for there was no need, and Grim was careful not to go where Ali Baba could not find him. We passed through acres of oleander-scrub into a valley twelve miles wide at its mouth, that narrowed gradually until the high red sandstone cliffs shut out the moonlight. It was like the mouth of hell, and suffocating, for the cliff-sides were giving off the heat they had sucked up through the day.

The surest sign that Ali Higg was either over-confident or seriously engaged elsewhere was that there was no guard in the ravine. Ten men properly placed could have destroyed us. Even the great Alexander of Macedon could not force that gorge, and suffered one of his worst defeats there. The Turks made the same mistake and tried to oust Lawrence in the Great War; but he simply overwhelmed them with a scratch brigade of partly armed Bedouins and women.

Grim called a halt at last where a dozen caves a hundred feet above the bottom of the gorge could be reached by a goat-track leading to a ledge. There was a rift in the side-wall there, making a pitch-dark corner where the camels could lie unseen and grumble to one another--safe enough until daylight, unless they should see ghosts and try to stampede for the open. Grim sent the women and Ayisha's four men up to the caves with only Narayan Singh to watch them, for there was no way of escape, except by that twelve-inch goat-track.

Then, because Ali Baba's sons and grandsons were nervous about the "old man their father," and because the one thing that more than all other circumstances combined could ruin our slim chance would be panic, Grim squatted on the sand in the gorge with the men all around him and began to tell stories.

Right there in the very jaws of death, within a mile of the lair of Ali Higg, in possession of two of the tyrant's wives, with an army at our rear that might at that minute be following old Ali Baba into the gorge to cut off our one possible retreat, he told them the old tales that Arabs love, and soothed them as if they were children.

That was the finest glimpse of Grim's real manhood I had experienced yet, although I could not see him for the darkness. You couldn't see any one. It was a voice in the night--strong, reassuring--telling to born thieves stories of the warm humanity of other thieves, whose accomplishments in the way of cool cheek and lawless altruism were hardly more outrageous than the task in front of us.

And he told them so well that even when a chill draft crept along the bottom of the gorge two hours before dawn, taking the place of the hot air that had ascended, and you could feel the shiver that shook the circle of listeners, they only drew closer and leaned forward more intently--almost as if he were a fire at which they warmed themselves.

But heavens! It seemed madness, nevertheless. We had no more pickets out than the enemy had. We were relying utterly on Grim's information that he had extracted from the women and the prisoners, and on his judgment based on that.

No doubt he knew a lot that he had not told us, for that is his infernal way of doing business; but neither that probability, nor his tales that so suited the Arab mind, nor the recollection of earlier predicaments in which his flair for solutions had been infallibly right, soothed my nerves much; and I nearly jumped out of my skin when a series of grunts and stumbling footfalls broke the stillness of the gorge behind us.

It sounded like ten weary camels being cursed by ten angry men, and I supposed at once that Ibrahim ben Ah had sent a detachment to investigate and that this was their advance-guard. Who else would dare to lift his voice in that way in the gorge? You could hear the words presently:

"Ill-bred Somali beast! Born among vermin in a black man's kraal! Allah give thee to the crows! Weary? What of it? What of my back, thou awkward earthquake! Thou plow-beast! A devil sit on thee! A devil drive thee! A devil eat thee!"

Whack! Whack!

"Oh my bones! My old bones!"

Mujrim was the first to recognize the voice. He got up quietly and stood in the gorge; and in another minute a blot of denser blackness that was a camel loomed above him, and he raised his hand to seize the head-rope. But the camel saw him first, and, realizing that the journey was over at last, flung itself to the ground with the abandon of a foundered dog, and lay with its neck stretched out straight and legs all straddled anyhow. Mujrim was just in time to catch his father, who was nearly as tired as the camel. It was pretty obvious at once that Jael's authority had failed badly when it came to exchanging camels.

The sons all surrounded the old man and made a fuss over him, laying him down on a sheepskin coat and chafing his stiff muscles, calling him brave names, rubbing his feet, patting his hands, praising him, while he swore at them each time they touched a sore spot.

They would not even give him a chance to hand over his letter to Grim, until at last he swore so savagely that Mujrim paid attention and took the letter out of the old man's waistcloth. It was in the same envelop in which the other had gone, unsealed, but with the thumb-mark of Ibrahim ben Ah imprinted on its face.

"To think that I, of all people, should fetch and carry for such dogs!" swore Ali Baba. "I asked for a good beast in exchange for mine, and they gave me this crow's meat, and laughed! May Allah change their faces! May the water of that oasis turn their bowels into stone!

"Aye, Jimgrim, they will stay there! They are glad enough to stay there. They are dogs that fear their master's whip. They are so afraid of him that I think if Ali Higg should bid them roast themselves alive the dogs would do it. May they roast a second time in hell for giving me that camel.

"Bah! What kind of sons have I? Are these the sons of my loins that let me parch? Is there no water-bag?"

Grim struck a match in the dark corner where the camels were; but all the envelop contained was a piece of jagged paper torn from the original letter, with Ibrahim ben Ah's thumb-mark done in ink made from gunpowder by way of ac-knowledgment. It meant, presumably, that instructions would be obeyed, and so far, good; we were not now in danger of trouble from that source.

But Ali Baba found his tongue again, and freed himself from his sons after he had drank about a quart of water.

"That Ibrahim ben Ah was puzzled," he said. "Allah! But the fool asked ques-tions; and by the Prophet's beard I lied in answer to him! Ho! What a string of lies! Who was I but a sheikh from El-Kalil bringing word to Ali Higg of the movements of a British force! In what way did I become the friend of Ali Higg? Was I not al-ways his friend! Was it not I who fed him when he first escaped from Egypt! Ho-ho-ho! Have I not been working for a year to gather men for him in El-Kalil! Have

I not made purchases in El-Kalil and El-Kudz for his wife Ayisha! *Il hamdulillah!*
My tongue was ready! May the lies rot the belly of the fool who ate them!

"But that was not all. He wanted to know other things--as, for instance, whether the other force of forty men is still at large, and if so who shall protect the women
in Petra.

"'For,' quoth he, `by Allah, there are men in the neighborhood who have felt
our Ali's heel, and who would not scruple to wreak vengeance if his back were altogether turned. Convey him my respectful homage, and bid him look to his rear,'
said Ibrahim ben Ah."

At that Grim called to Narayan Singh, who came down the goat-track like a
landslide. You mustn't whistle your man in those parts, or the Arabs will say the
devil has defiled your mouth.

"Ask Jael Higg to come here."

"A word first, Jimgrim sahib! While I watched, those women talked. Jael, the
older one, offered Ayisha forgiveness if she would obey henceforth; but Ayisha
gave her only hard words, saying that in a day or so it will be seen whose cock crows
loudest. So Jael called to two of the men who have been with Ayisha all this time,
and they squatted in the mouth of her cave. As it was very dark I crept quite close
and listened. She bade them watch their chance and run to Ali Higg.

"'If he is ill and angry, never mind,' she said. `If he beats you, never mind. He
will reward you afterward. Bid him, as he values life,' she said, `call in those forty
men whom he would send to punish the Beni Aroun people. Tell him I am a prisoner, but those forty are enough to turn the tables until Ibrahim ben Ah can come.
A camel must leave in a hurry for Ibrahim ben Ah at the oasis, and bring him and
all the men back to straighten this affair.'

"She promised them money and promotion for success, and sure death for failure!"

"Good!" said Grim, turning to me. "You see? It always pays to stage a close-up
in a game like this. We've caught our friend Ali Higg between soup and fish."

"Get in quick, then, and kidnap him," I urged.

"Man alive," he answered, "we've no kind of right to do that. Bring her down,"
he told Narayan Singh, "and then have Mujrim tie those four men of Ayisha's so
they've no chance to escape."

Jael Higg came down in a livid passion--altogether too near home to enjoy taking secondhand orders from an Indian in the dark. She was still less amused when she discovered that Grim knew her little scheme.

"Well, Jael," he said, "you weren't quite frank with me after all, were you? Which will you do now--stay in that hole up there with a double guard, or come into Petra with us and behave yourself?"

For, I should say, a whole minute, she did not answer. You could not tell in the dark, but I think she was fighting back tears, and too proud to betray it.

"I'm your prisoner," she hissed at last. "Do what you like, and take the consequences."

"I'll put you to no indignity, Jael, if you'll play fair."

"My God! What? Are you mad, or am I? What are you going to do with Ali Higg?"

"Make friends with him."

"You swear that?"

"Sure."

She was silent for another minute.

"Very well," she said at last. "I'll do my best."

"Accepted," answered Grim. "Now--bring down Ayisha--fetch out the camels--mount--and forward all!"

We went forward just as dawn was breaking, and I believe every man Jack of us except Grim had his heart in his teeth. Grim was likely too busy conning over the plan in his head to feel afraid, that being, as far as I could ever tell, the one lone advantage of being leader, just as the capacity to drive out fear by steady thinking is as good a reason as exists for placing a man in command.

Nobody knows how old Petra is, but it was a thriving city when Abraham left Ur of the Chaldees, and for a full five thousand years it has had but that one entrance, through a gorge that narrows finally until only one loaded camel at a time can pass. Army after army down the centuries have tried to storm the place, and failed, so that even the invincible Alexander and the Romans had to fall back on the arts of friendship to obtain the key. We, the last invaders, came as friends, if only Grim could persuade the tyrant to believe it.

The sun rose over the city just as we reached the narrowest part of the gut,

Grim leading, and its first rays showed that we were using the bed of a watercourse for a road. Exactly in front of us, glimpsed through a twelve-foot gap between cliffs six hundred feet high, was a sight worth going twice that distance, running twice that risk, to see--a rose-red temple front, carved out of the solid valley wall and glistening in the opalescent hues of morning.

Not even Burkhardt, who was the first civilized man to see the place in a thousand years, described that temple properly; because you can't. It is huge--majestic--silent--empty--aglow with all the prism colors in the morning sun. And it seems to think.

It takes you so by surprise when you first see it that in face of that embodied mystery of ancient days your brain won't work, and you want to sit spellbound. But Grim had done our thinking for us, so that we were not the only ones surprised. Such was the confidence of safety that those huge walls and the narrow entrance to the place inspire that Ali Higg had set only four men to keep the gate; and they slept with their weapons beside them, never believing that strangers would dare essay that ghost-haunted ravine by night.

They were pounced on and tied almost before their eyes were open; and, catching sight of Jael Higg first, and getting only a glimpse of Grim, they rather naturally thought their chief had caught them napping; so they neither cried out nor made any attempt to defend themselves; and presently, when they discovered their mistake, the fear of being crucified for having slept on duty kept them dumb.

Grim led the way straight to that amazing temple, and we invaded it, camels and all, off-loading the camels inside in a hurry and then driving them out again to lie down in the wide porch between the columns and the temple wall. The porch was so vast that even all our string of camels did not crowd it.

The main part of the interior was a perfect cube of forty feet, all hand-hewn from the cliff, and there were numerous rooms leading out of it that had once been occupied by the priests of Isis, but "the lion and the lizard" had lived in them since their day. We put the prisoners, including Ayisha's four men, in one room under guard.

That much was hardly accomplished when the spirit of our seventeen thieves reacted to their surroundings, and all the advantage of our secret arrival was suddenly undone. Half of them had gone outside to tie the camels, under Ali Baba's watchful eye; and it was he, as a matter of fact, who started it. From inside we heard a regular din of battle commencing--loud shouts and irregular rifle-fire--and I followed Grim out in a hurry.

There was no enemy in sight. Old Ali Baba was busy reloading his rifle fifty paces away in front of the temple door, facing us with his sons, in a semicircle around him, and they were shooting at something over our heads. Grim laughed rather bitterly.

"My mistake," he said. "I ought to have thought of that."

So I went out to see.

Surmounting the temple front, at least a hundred feet above the pavement and perfectly inaccessible, was a beautifully carved stone urn surmounting a battered image of some god or goddess. It was in shadow, because the cliff wall, from which the temple had been carved, overhung it; so it was peculiarly difficult to hit, even at that range; but they were all firing away at it as if Ali Higg and all his men were hidden behind the thing. There was no particular need to stop them, for they had made noise enough already to awake the very slumbering bones of Petra. Ali Baba advised me to shoot too, and I asked him why.

"To burst the thing."

"But why?"

"That we make a profit from this venture."

"How?"

He paused to reload once more. He had already fired away about fifteen cartridges.

"Allah! The very dogs of El-Kalil have heard of Pharaoh's treasure."

"I am neither a dog," said I, "nor an inhabitant of El-Kalil, for which Allah for his thoughtfulness be praised! Tell me what you and the dogs know."

"This place was the treasury of Pharaoh, King of Egypt, a bad king and an unbeliever, whom may Allah curse! In that urn are his gold and rubies. If we can crack it they will come tumbling down and we shall all be rich."

"Mashallah! You believe that? Why haven't Ali Higg and his men cracked it, then?"

"Shu halalk?[26] I have told you Pharaoh was an evil king. He was in league

---

26   What chatter is this?

with devils and bewitched the place. The devils guard it. May Allah twist their tails! Look--see! We shoot, but the bullets miss the mark each time!"

"Perhaps you haven't prayed enough to exorcize the devils?" I suggested, and he dropped the butt of his rifle on the ground to consider the proposition.

"Out of the mouth of an unbeliever has come wisdom before now," he said. "There may be truth in that."

And he called all his sons and grandsons there and then to spread their mats and pray toward Mecca, performing the prescribed ablutions first with water from one of the goatskin bags.

Well, there wasn't any further use in trying to keep our movements secret. Grim beckoned me to where he stood beside Narayan Singh, with Ayisha looking mischievous in the gloom behind them, and issued final instructions.

"Present my compliments and these gifts to Ali Higg--I'm busy at prayer, re-member--and say how greatly honored we feel to have escorted his wife across the desert. If he asks where her four men are, tell him I'll bring them later. Be sure and make me out a great sheikh, and say I heard he is sick, so sent my *hakim* in advance to give him relief; then do your best for him, if he'll let you--after Ayisha has done her worst," he added in a whisper. "Don't forget you're a ***darwaish.*** The more you jaw religion the better the old rascal will like you. See you soon. So long!"

So Narayan Singh and I, followed by Ayisha and two of Ali Baba's sons, left that ancient temple bearing the medicine-chest as well as presents, and I hope the others did not feel as scared as I did.

CHAPTER XII

"Yet I Forgot to Speak of the Twenty Aeroplanes!"

You can expect anything, of course, of Arabs. People who will pitch black cotton tents in the scorching sun, and live in them in preference to gorgeous cool stone temples because of the devils and ghosts that they believe to haunt those habitable splendors, will believe anything at all except the truth, and act in any way except reasonably. So I tried to believe it was all right to be unreasonable too.

You would think, wouldn't you, that a man who had set himself up to be the holy terror of a country-side and put his heel on the necks of all the tribes for miles around, would have made use at least of the caves and tombs to strengthen his position. There were thousands of them all among those opal-colored cliffs, to say nothing of ruined buildings; yet not one was occupied. Ayisha had told most of the truth when she said in El-Kalil that her people lived in tents.

We walked down the paved street of a city between oleander bushes that had forced themselves up between the cracks, toward an enormous open amphitheater hewn by the Romans out of a hillside, with countless tiers of ruined stone seats rising one above the other like giant steps.

In the center of that the tents were pitched, and the only building in use was a great half-open cave on another hillside, in which Ayisha told us Ali Higg himself lived, overlooking the entire camp and directing its destinies.

On the top of the mountain in front of us was the tomb of Aaron, Moses' brother. On another mountain farther off stood a great crusader castle all in ruins; and to left and right were endless remains of civilization that throve when the British were living in mud-and-wattle huts. The dry climate had preserved it all; but there was water enough; it only needed the labor of a thousand men to remake a city of it.

We avoided the amphitheater with its hundreds of tents pitched inside and all about it, because Ayisha said the women would come running out to greet her, and she did not desire that any more than we did. So we turned to the right, and started up a flight of steps nearly a mile long that led to an ancient place of sacrifice; two hundred yards up that the track turned off that led to Ali Higg's cavern.

It was there, where the broken steps and sidetrack met, that the first men came hurrying to meet us and blocked our way--four of them, active as goats, and looking fierce enough to scare away twice their number. But they recognized Ayisha, and stood aside at once to let us pass, showing her considerable gruff respect and asking a string of questions, which she countered with platitudes. They did not follow us, but stayed on guard at the corner, as if the meeting between Ali Higg and his wife were something to keep from prying eyes.

So the far-famed Ali Higg was alone in his great cave when we reached it, sitting near the entrance propped on skins and cushions with a perfect armory of weapons on the floor beside him. The interior was hung with fine Bokhara embroideries, and every inch of the floor was covered with rugs.

There was another cave opening into that in which he sat; and it, too, was richly decorated; but the sound of women's voices that we heard came from a third cave around the corner of the cliff wall, not connected. Ali Higg was apparently in no mood for female company--or any other kind.

In the shadow of the overhanging rock he looked so like Grim it was laughable. He was a caricature of our man, with all the refinement and humor subtly changed into irritable anger. He looked as if he would scream if you touched him, and no wonder; for the back of the poor fellow's neck, half hidden by the folds of his head-cloth, was a perfect mess of boils that made every movement of his head an agony.

His eyes were darker than Grim's, and blazed as surely no white man's ever did; and his likeness to Grim was lessened by the fact that he had not been shaved for a day or two, and the sparse black hair coarsened the outline of his chin and jaw. In spite of his illness he had not laid aside the bandolier that crossed his breast, nor the two daggers tucked into his waist-cloth. And he laid his hand on a modern British Army rifle the minute he caught sight of us.

Narayan Singh and I both bowed and, after greeting him with the proper so-norous blessing, stood aside to let Ayisha approach. We should have demeaned ourselves in his eyes, and hers as well, if we had walked behind her. He nodded to us curtly, and almost smiled at her; but that one wry twist of his lips was his nearest approach to pleasantry that morning.

She knelt and kissed his hands and feet, waiting to speak until she was spoken to; and he did not speak to her at all, but signed to her with a tap on the head and a gesture to take her place on the rug behind him. Then at a motion from me Ali Baba's two sons brought forward the presents and the medicine-chest, setting them down before him in the cave-mouth.

The presents were pretty good, I thought. I would not have minded owning them myself; but he eyed them dully. There was a set of Solingen razors, marked in Arabic with the days of the week; a cloak of blue-and-white-striped cloth, fit for any prince of Bedouins; and an ormolu clock with a gong inside it that would have graced the chimneypiece of a Brooklyn boarding-house.

"Mar'haba!"[27] he said at last, by way of acknowledging our existence, after he had stared at the presents for about two minutes sourly; and I took that for permission to say my little piece.

So I delivered Grim's message, saying that he was a most God-fearing and hard-fighting sheikh from Palestine, who had had the honor to escort his mightiness' wife to Petra, and now, learning of the illness of the famous Lion of Petra, who might Allah bless for ever, rather than postpone his devotions had sent me, his **ha-kim,** schooled in medicine at Lahore University, and a **darwaish** to boot, to offer such relief as my modest skill might compass.

That was a long speech to get off in Arabic for a comparative beginner. I rather expected him to smile or say something pleasant in return, but he didn't.

"By Allah, you have come to poison me!" he growled. "All **hakims** are alike. There was an Egyptian tried it a month ago. Look yonder on the ledge, where his skull hangs. May devils burn his soul!"

It was easy enough to look shocked at that suggestion. He had the drop on me for one thing; and, for another, Ayisha was whispering to him, and I couldn't guess whether she was betraying me or not. It turned out that that young woman

27   Greeting

was much too bent on swapping owners to do anything but smooth our path; but I wasn't so sure of that then as Narayan Singh seemed to be, and as, for that matter, Grim was too.

But he seemed to grow a little less irascible, until she leaned too close to him and touched his neck. Then he went off like a pent-up volcano, and cursed her until she shuddered; and her fright gave him no satisfaction, because he could not turn his head to look at her.

"Where is this cursed person?" he demanded, meaning Grim, of course.

"He rests at the treasury of Pharaoh," said I, hoping that as Narayan Singh and I both stood exactly in front of him he might not catch sight of Grim's movements in the valley below.

"How did he enter Petra without my leave?" he demanded.

I took a long pause, for that was an awkward question. I could not very well admit that Grim had seized and imprisoned his watchmen. But Narayan Singh strode into the breach.

"The Lion's jackals slept," he announced in a voice of righteous indignation. "There was none to give our great Sheikh Jimgrim as much as Allah's blessing. Nevertheless, he sends these presents."

Without answering that Ali Higg clapped his hands twice, and a woman came around the corner from a near-by cave. By her bearing she was either a junior wife or a concubine, and she greeted Ayisha like a sister with a great pow-wow of blessing and reply. But Ali Higg cut all that short. He was no sentimentalist.

"Find Shammas Abdul," he ordered her. "Order him to take camel and meet the men returning from the Ben Aroun raid. Let him bid them hurry. Go!"

She obeyed on the run. There was discipline in that man's camp, as long as he was looking. But Ayisha followed the woman out, and whether she herself found Shammas Abdul, or whether she contrived to pervert the junior wife, Grim presently became aware of that move to summon forth men, and governed himself accordingly.

For about a minute Ali Higg fixed baleful eyes on me.

"You are a Shia!" he snapped suddenly. "A Persian! A cursed heretic!"

A look of pained surprise was the best retort I could accomplish; but Narayan Singh came to the rescue again. He thumped a fist on his chest as if it were a drum, and glared indignantly.

"Would I, a Pathan of the Orakzai, demean myself by being servant to a Persian?" he demanded. "Lo! We bring gifts. What manner of desert man are you that reward us with insults!"

"Peace!" I said. "Peace!" remembering the Sikh's counsel about the middle course I should pursue. "The Lion is sick. May Allah take pity on him!"

Narayan Singh growled in his beard by way of submitting to the mild rebuke, and Ali Higg--a little bit impressed perhaps--proceeded to question me on doctrine and theology, showing a zeal for splitting hairs that would have done credit to a Cairo *m'allim.* But I had had lots of instruction on those points, and in fact surprised him with a trite fanaticism equal to his own, ending with a statement that whoever did not believe every article and precept of the Sunni faith not only was damned forever beyond hope, but should be despatched in a hurry to face the dreadful consequences.

His eyes softened considerably at that; and for the moment I think he almost approved of me, in spite of the foreign accent that must have grated on his ears, and his national dislike of any one who hailed from India. He actually told both of us to be seated, and clapped his hands again. Another woman came, looking dreadfully afraid of him.

"Coffee!" he ordered.

We sat down on the ledge of rock in front of him, for although it was hardly wise to seem too deferent, it would have been most unwise to move away and give him an unobstructed view of the valley, where Grim might be in sight or might not be. Our job was to gain time.

He did not say a word until the coffee came, beyond swearing scandalously when he moved his head and the boils hurt.

"O Allah, may Your neck hurt You as mine does me!"

I thought that pretty good for such a hard-and-fast doctrinaire, but it was almost mild compared to some of his other remarks.

The woman brought the coffee on a tray in little silver cups--as good and as well served as if our host were a Cairene pasha; but our irascible host took none, for Ayisha called out and warned him not to, saying it would heat his boils.

She came like the wife of Heber the Kenite, who slew Sisera, "bringing forth butter in a lordly dish." She held in both hands a marvelous Persian rose-bowl half filled with clabber, saying she had prepared it for her lord herself, and offered it to him on bended knees.

I could not see her face, for her back was toward me and she had her shawl over her head; but I thought of that little vial of croton oil Narayan Singh had given her instead of poison, and the Sikh caught my eye meaningly.

Ali Higg was pleased to condescend. He took the bowl in both hands, muttered a blessing, and drank deep, swallowing about half the stuff before he noticed its strange flavor. Then he flung the priceless bowl away from him, smashing it to atoms, and picked up his rifle to take an aim at Ayisha.

"By Allah, the bint[28] has poisoned me!"

She screamed and ran. He fired, but she was already past the corner, and the bullet grazed the rock. Moreover, croton oil is a drastic cathartic, and waits on no man's convenience. He dropped the rifle, groaned--and I would rather not set down quite all the rest.

Sufficient that it gave Narayan Singh and me our opportunity. It made him too weak to resist, and we took care of him. I let him go on believing he was poisoned, and gave him harmless doses that he presently believed had saved his life; so that even the tyrannical fanatic felt a kind of gratitude.

Held like a baby in the Sikh's enormous arms with no less than half a dozen terrified women looking on--for they had all run one way while Ayisha ran the other--he slowly recovered control of his emotions, while the women loudly praised my medicinal skill.

And since I knew almost nothing at all of medicine, and therefore could say anything I chose without feeling guilty--like the fellow on a soapbox who harangues a crowd on politics--I told him he must have the boils lanced there and then, or otherwise the poison might get to them and inflame them beyond all hope.

I suppose the men who had met us at the corner of the great flight of steps did not come and interrupt because they had had enough of his temper for one morning and did not choose to sample it again uninvited. The rifle-shot did not bring them, because it was nothing new for him to vent displeasure by shooting at folk; and if there were a corpse, and it had not fallen over the cliff or been kicked over, they

---

28   Literally girl; about as respectful as the word "skirt" would be if used of one's wife.

would come and remove it when ordered, but certainly not sooner.

Ali Higg has strength enough left to assure me that if I killed him he would wait for me in the next world and settle the account there. I told him what was perfectly true, that I would rather lose my hand than kill him, so he added that if I hurt him more than was reasonable four camels should be told off afterward to hurt me.

Seeing he was to be sole judge of what was reasonable pain, and having no means of guessing whether Grim was still alive and able to protect me, I decided to give him a hypodermic, and put a shot into his arm that would have quieted a *must* elephant. Maybe I rather overdid that, but as I have no medical diploma nobody can call me to account.

And the operation was successful, if unpleasant. I used one of the presentation razors.

Then Grim came striding up the mountain-ledge, with Ali Baba and all the rest of the gang at his tail, but no sign anywhere of Jael Higg. He stood and boomed out a sonorous Arab blessing; and if ever a man felt and looked like a trapped wild beast it was that Lord of the Limits of the Desert and Lion of Petra, Ali Higg.

However, Narayan Singh and I had played our part and got him weak enough; he could not even jump to grab his rifle. The rest was clearly up to Grim, who looked in no hurry at all.

He stood in the cave entrance with the light behind him, turning slightly side-wise to let Ali Higg see him in profile. The Lion's jaw dropped. Grim's very head-dress was striped like Ali Higg's. His cloak was the same color. He had been dressed rather differently when I last saw him, so he must have been doing some pretty careful spy-work.

Of course, a close examination showed a dozen differences between the two men, but in his weak state following that drastic physic and the operation Ali Higg believed for a moment that he saw his own ghost! One or two of the women checked a scream, which helped matters, and the others shrank into a corner, staring with wild eyes. One woman laughed, but not from amusement.

"*Salamun alaik,* O Ali Higg!" said Grim after a full minute's silence.

"*Wa alaik issalam!* Who are you, in the name of Allah?"

Instead of answering Grim strode in, and Ali Baba lined up his sons across the cave-mouth. Unless Grim had left undone some precaution in the camp below it looked as if we had the Lion caged to rights, and you could tell by the look in Ali Baba's usually mild old eyes that there would have been short shrift for somebody if his advice were taken. For a moment I caught sight of Ayisha peering timidly between the end man and the wall--to see, I suppose, whether the Lion was dead yet--but the minute I caught her eye she disappeared.

Grim stooped down over Ali Higg, who was sprawling on his stomach on a Persian rug.

"Has my *hakim* relieved Your Honor's pain?" he asked.

The Lion managed to sit upright. Three of the women piled cushions behind him and ran back again to their corner.

"Who are you in my likeness?"

"A friend, *inshallah*," answered Grim.

He squatted down cross-legged on the mat in front of him; for though the Lion's neck was pretty nicely bandaged and the hypodermic had not lost its power, yet it hurt him quite a little to look up.

"I had three brothers, but thou art none of them. I had one son, but neither art thou he. In the name of the All-Knowing, name thyself!"

"I am he," said Grim, "who brought Your Honor's wife from El-Kalil."

"Oh! And a million curses on the bint! She tried within the hour to poison me. But for this Indian of thine I were a dead man now. Stay! Send for her!"

He clapped his hands.

"Let her be flung over the cliff. Go bring her!" But nobody moved to do his bidding, and it dawned on him a second time that he was cornered. He wasn't a man who took such a discovery mildly.

"Ayisha shall be dealt with at the proper time!" he snarled. "I have not accepted those gifts. Take them up! You who have entered Petra without my leave shall account to my men presently. Thereafter we will talk of gifts."

"Which men?" Grim asked him blandly. "Surely not the forty and four who went to raid the Beni Aroun? Nay, I took the liberty of sending them a message signed with Your Honor's seal. They will not come for a day or two, so we can make friends undisturbed."

"Shu halalk? With my seal?"

"With Your Honor's seal. Observe; I have it."

"Then--then--Where is she into whose hands I gave it?"

That was the first sign that Ali Higg had given of the slightest affection for any one. His face looked ghastly at the thought of losing that strange, half-western wife of his.

He had called Ayisha by her name in front of strangers, out of disrespect. Jael he would not name, even when confronted by the proof that she had broken trust and lost his precious seal.

"I took another liberty," said Grim. "I sent word by messenger, who bore a letter sealed with that same seal, to Ibrahim ben Ah. He will neither raid El-Maan nor return to Petra."

"He is defeated?" asked the Lion, dumbfounded. "And she--is she a prisoner?"

Grim did not answer either question.

"And I met a man named Yussuf. You know him?"

"Naam." (Yes).

"He has been lying to Your Honor. He has said that the British are helpless. He brought Your Honor a report from Palestine that was a skein of falsehood hung up on little pegs of truth. He told you the British are not able to defend themselves, he knowing better; for he is one of those men who say always what the hearer would like to hear."

"What has that to do with thee?" demanded Ali Higg.

He was looking about him furtively, and Narayan Singh picked up his rifle off the rug and stood it against the wall. Grim turned toward Ali Baba.

"Bring Yussuf!" he ordered.

The ranks opened, and Yussuf was thrust forward into the cave, where he stood looking like a felon awaiting sentence.

"Did you speak the truth, or did you lie to the Lion of Petra?" Grim demanded.

"Who am I that should know the truth of such matters?" the man whined, his voice squeaking like a cart-wheel. "I obeyed. I looked. I asked. Perhaps I did not understand all I saw and what was told me."

"Is the Lion of Petra with ten-score fighting men able to stand against the British with twenty thousand?" Grim asked him.

"Inshallah. The Lion is brave. Who knows? Yet I forgot to speak of the twenty

aeroplanes at Ludd, each having ten bombs of a hundred pounds weight that could make short work in an hour or two of ten score men."

"Why don't they come?" snarled Ali Higg.

"They take no delight in slaying the women and children," answered Grim. "Those black tents below there would be an easy mark to aim at; but who would gain? It is better that peace were kept."

"Throw that Yussuf over the cliff!" commanded Ali Higg.

But once more nobody moved to obey him, and Yussuf had the indecency to smirk, for which Grim cursed him with whiplash sarcasm.

Then Ali Higg put both hands before his face and prayed aloud:

"O Allah, Lord of mercies and of wisdom and rebuke, if I am in the hands of enemies and she who was the mother of good plans is taken away from me, have I not, nevertheless, smitten the heretic in thy name and raised thy banner over Petra? Give me, then, wisdom, that I deal with these men and confound thy enemies. *La Allah illa Allah!*"

He dropped his hands and looked up with a hard, fanatical frenzy in his eyes. But they changed almost instantly. The ranks of Ali Baba's men opened once more; and Jael Higg stepped through, dressed like a fighting Bedouin, bandolier and all. Grim had even let her have a rifle and cartridges. As he promised, he had put her to no indignity.

CHAPTER XIII

"There is a Trick to Ruling!"

Don't you hate a story with a moral in it? I do. This is an immoral story. And, remember, I said in the beginning that it had no end, but was no more than an episode in the career of Ali Higg. I would have liked to tell it from his viewpoint setting down what he thought of this unexpected stick thrown in his wheel, omitting most of the bad language for the censor's sake.

His first thought was that Jael had returned from the raid with a hundred and forty men. You could tell that by the light in his eyes, even before he spoke.

"Allah reward you; you come in time! Have Ayisha and that Yussuf thrown over the cliff. Praised be Allah, I shall be obeyed at last!"

It was his worst shock yet when even Jael did not start at once to carry out his order. Instead, she sat down on the rug, so that she and Ali Higg and Grim formed a triangle.

"O Lion of Petra," she said--for it would not have been manners to call him by his right name in front of strangers--"what was written has come to pass, and my foreboding was a true one. If we had let the tribes at El-Maan be, and if you had kept those forty men instead of sending them to raid the Beni Aroun, this could not have happened. Now twenty men have cornered us, while Ibrahim ben Ah eats up provisions to no purpose, sitting idly in the desert."

"Then the El-Maan men were not scattered to the winds?" groaned Ali Higg. "O Allah, may shame devour you as it tortures me! Those dogs will have looted a train and will say that Ali Higg no longer dares interfere! The sun rises, but it sets at evening, since Allah wills; but is my day so short?"

"By no means," answered Grim. "The El-Maan men saw me and believed I was the Lion of Petra. I forbade the looting of the train, and Your Honor's wife Ayisha went to El-Maan to enforce obedience by her presence.

"Later they saw me start for Petra when the train had passed; and now they will learn that Ibrahim ben Ah with seven score men is bivouacking in the desert. The world is round, O Ali Higg, so that where in one place it seems dark in another they say the sun is rising."

"In Allah's name, who art thou?" asked the Lion.

"James Schuyler Grim. Men call me Jimgrim."

"Allah! *Wallahi haida fasl!*[29] Not he who fought under Lawrence against the Turks? *Wallah!* I fought on the other side, but we all feared Lawrence and admired him so that not a man would try to capture him, although Djemal Pasha put a great price on his head. And you were known far and wide as his man! There was a price on your head too--dead or alive--five thousand pounds Turkish--well I remember it. By the beard of the Prophet, you might have come here as a friend, O Jimgrim!"

Grim laughed.

"I come here as a friend in any case," he answered. *"Khajjaltni bima'rufak!*[30] You brought back a woman to poison me!"

And this is where the immorality comes in. I told a lie, and don't regret it. Nor did Grim regret it; and he backed me up. And Narayan Singh supported both of us.

The lie was my own idea entirely, invented on the spur of the moment; and afterward, when old Ali Baba named me The "Father of Lies" on the strength of it I felt extremely proud, as he intended that I should do. The lie worked.

I said:

"O Ali Higg, men said of you that you are a fierce man, swift in wrath and slow to take advice. And others said that you are sick with burning boils; yet who shall go into the Lion's den and heal him? And Ayisha said to me:

"'Thou art a *hakim,* yet he will never listen to thee. But he is my lord, and shall I see him linger in agony? Give me a potion that will weaken him. Then in his weakness he will call for help, and thou shalt heal the boils. And afterward that which is written shall come to pass. If in great wrath because I mixed the potion in his drink he shall have me slain, nevertheless the Lion will be whole again; and who

---

29   By Allah, this is a strange happening.
30   You shame me with your friendship!

am I compared to him?' So said the lady Ayisha."

I know Grim would have given a hundred dollars for leave to laugh then right out in meeting; but he kept a straight face, and he had so contrived to make Jael Higg afraid of him that though she looked scandalized she held her tongue. And Narayan Singh, as I said, supported me.

"These words are true, O Lion of Petra," he boomed out. "I heard the lady Ayisha speak, and it was I who put the little vial in her hands. By the beard of the Prophet I swear the words are true."

But as he is a Sikh, and therefore believes that the prophet of El-Islam was a liar and impostor, with a beard as fit to be dishonored as his fiery creed, perhaps his perjury was scarcely technical. Anyhow, I am not the recording angel. And Grim said, being a more cautious liar than the rest of us:

"Therefore, O Lion of Petra, mercy is due to the lady Ayisha, seeing that the end in view was good, although the means were questionable."

But Jael Higg looked daggers at her lord. She had made up her mind to reduce that establishment by one at least; and Ali Higg, looking in her eyes, read what all polygamous husbands have had to face ever since the day when Abraham was forced to drive out Hagar into the wilderness. So he pronounced one of those Solomon-like judgments that are the secret of a man's rule over men in that land, granting to each contender the whole of what he asked, yet having his own way in the bargain.

"I find she is not worthy of death," he said, "since she played a trick that brought me comfort. Yet I will not endure a woman's tricks, nor condone the offense. I divorce her. Before witnesses I say she is divorced."

It's a simple affair in that land, isn't it?

But there were matters not so simple to attend to, and Grim saw fit to waste no further time.

"I said I come as a friend," he resumed.

"I heard it!" the Lion answered dryly.

"Without boasting, I have saved you from destruction, while delivering your purchases from El-Kalil. And I have done your name no harm, but good on the country-side."

"Allah! How have you saved me from destruction?"

"By preventing that unwise raid on El-Maan."

"Wallahi! Do you think my men could not have accomplished it?"

"Maybe. Do you think the British would be fools enough to let that go unpunished? The El-Maan people would surely have appealed to them. Aeroplanes would have been sent to bomb you out of Petra. Can you fight aeroplanes?"

"The British do not pretend to rule on this side of the Jordan," the Lion retorted.

"No. Do you want them to pretend to?"

"Allah forbid!"

"Then take a friend's advice, O Ali Higg, and keep the peace here rather than make war."

"That is good advice; but will the British make a treaty with me?"

"No," Grim answered, smiling. "By that they would recognize you as a ruler, which they will not do until they surely know you rule."

"Mashallah! How shall men know that I am a ruler unless I make war and enforce my will?"

"Have I made war on you?" asked Grim. "Have I disarmed you, or killed one man? Yet I enforce my will, as you shall see."

"By a trick! You played a trick on me, or otherwise--"

"There is a trick to ruling," answered Grim.

"By the beard of the Prophet, that is true! But show me a trick that can defeat eight hundred men. The Sheikh of Abu Lissan plans to come against me. Those El-Mann dogs had heard of it, and so had the Beni Aroun; therefore I planned to crush them first before dealing with Abu Lissan. Show me a trick that can defeat the Abu Lissan men, and surely I will call thee friend!"

"Suppose we make a bargain, then," said Grim.

"Taib. I am ready."

"Giving pledges for fulfilment."

"You mean I shall give pledges to the British?"

"Hardly," Grim answered. "If they took a pledge from you that would be like signing a treaty, wouldn't it? I have no authority to sign a treaty. This must be a bargain between me and thee."

"Taib."

"It is known," said Grim, "that you have money on deposit with the Bank of

Egypt."

"A lie! A lie!" snapped Ali Higg. "Who said it?"

"Fifty thousand pounds in gold was the exact amount, deposited at six percent, and interest to be compounded every half-year," said Grim. "And because the Koran denounces usury by Moslems, and you are a pious man--and also perhaps because of the risk attached to using your name in the matter--your wife Jael's name was used. Nevertheless, your seal was used at the time as a check on her. Now, at a word from me the British would impound that money, interest and all."

"A murrian on them! But you spoke of being friends?"

"And of a pledge between you and me. In proof that I speak as a friend, though I had your seal I have returned it."

Jael Higg confirmed that by displaying it in the hollow of her hand.

"You can't possibly prevent a message from me reaching British territory," Grim went on. "A letter is written already, and you don't know which man has it. You are not my prisoner. I intend to leave you free and unharmed. It is possible you might attack me when I go, and kill me and some of my men; but the rest would escape. And then would come aeroplanes, and you would never see that money in the Bank of Egypt."

The Lion blinked away steadily, looking so absurdly like Grim in some respects, and so utterly unlike him in character nevertheless, that it looked like plus opposing minus, or a strong man tempted by his baser self.

"Therefore," continued Grim, "if you will promise me to raid no more villages I will undertake to deal with the Sheikh of Abu Lissan. But as a pledge, Jael and you must sign and seal a letter to the Bank of Egypt stipulating that the fifty thousand pounds shall not be withdrawn for three years. As long as you keep your promise that money of yours shall be safe, with no questions asked as to how you came by it; for I shall not say a word about it to the British Government, making only a sealed report, which shall be locked away and never opened unless you break the bargain."

"And at the end of three years?"

"Who knows?" Grim answered. "The years are on the lap of Allah. By then we may all be dead, or you may be king, or may be weary of politics--who knows?"

"And if I refuse?"

"Aeroplanes!"

"But how shall I believe you?"

"Do I not pledge my life?" Grim answered. "I have said that I will go to Abu Lissan."

"Allah! Why don't you send the aeroplanes to Abu Lissan? Blot the dogs out! Destroy them! Why not?"

"Would it not be easier to send them here?" asked Grim. "This is only part way. You, who found it easier to crush the smaller first, tell me why the aeroplanes should not come first to Petra!"

"Wallahi! I wish I had aeroplanes!"

"But you haven't. Choose now: Will you make that bargain with me, or shall I go straight back from here to Palestine and make my report to the administrator? Never doubt that I can get back; I know where your men are, and I know the desert trails as well as you do. You and your few men that you have here and the women might attack us in the Wady Musa,[31] but I would prevent that by taking you and Jael with me until we reached the open."

"You talk boldly," the Lion sneered. "If you think you can take us with you that far then why not to Jerusalem? The words of a boaster are a mask of doubt. Hah! Take us to Jerusalem! Why not?"

"Because then," Grim answered, "there would be ten-score cutthroats at large without a leader who can hold them. One Lion can keep a bargain, but ten score jackals would ruin a country-side."

Ali Higg turned that over in his mind for five full minutes, like a chess player refusing to admit that he is mated. But there wasn't a move left to him, and Jael went closer on her knees to whisper advice in his ear.

"I agree," he said at last. "As Allah is my witness, I agree. Let us be friends, O Jimgrim!"

Grim shook hands with him and offered him a cigarette, while Ali Baba's men outside the cave sent up a great shout of victory. Then to Ali Higg's inexpressible delight Mahommed started to sing the Akbar song, and they all roared the chorus:

"Akbar! Akbar! Akbar Ali Higg!"

The song put everybody in good temper, so that when Jael wrote out a letter

---

31 The name of the valley that leads into Petra

to the bank at Grim's dictation Ali Higg affixed the seal to it without a murmur and ordered food supplied at once to all Grim's men; and we had a feast up there on the ledge outside the cave--in sight of the very spot where Amaziah, King of Israel, once hurled ten thousand of his enemies into the gorge below--that, in some respects, was the most enjoyable I ever shared.

But Grim was not the man to spoil success by lingering in what might yet turn into a trap. He who sups with the devil should not sit long at the feast; and I warned you this was a story without an end to it.

There is the lady Ayisha, and what became of her, and the account of when and in what way the Lion kept his bargain. Well, have you heard of those tale-tellers in the East, who sit under a village tree with the menfolk all around them? They work up to the climax, and then pause, and pass the begging-bowl for whatever the tale is worth. I fear those masters of inducement would mock me as a tyro for having already told too much before the pause!

The Codes Of Hammurabi And Moses
W. W. Davies

QTY

The discovery of the Hammurabi Code is one of the greatest achievements of archaeology, and is of paramount interest, not only to the student of the Bible, but also to all those interested in ancient history...

Religion   **ISBN:** *1-59462-338-4*   **Pages:132**

MSRP $12.95

The Theory of Moral Sentiments
Adam Smith

QTY

This work from 1749. contains original theories of conscience amd moral judgment and it is the foundation for systemof morals.

Philosophy   ISBN: *1-59462-777-0*   **Pages:536**

MSRP $19.95

Jessica's First Prayer
Hesba Stretton

QTY

In a screened and secluded corner of one of the many railway-bridges which span the streets of London there could be seen a few years ago, from five o'clock every morning until half past eight, a tidily set-out coffee-stall, consisting of a trestle and board, upon which stood two large tin cans, with a small fire of charcoal burning under each so as to keep the coffee boiling during the early hours of the morning when the work-people were thronging into the city on their way to their daily toil...

Pages:84

Childrens   ISBN: *1-59462-373-2*   *MSRP $9.95*

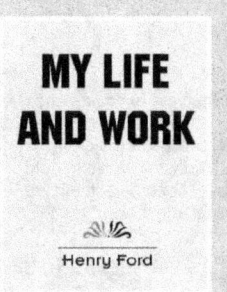

My Life and Work
Henry Ford

QTY

Henry Ford revolutionized the world with his implementation of mass production for the Model T automobile. Gain valuable business insight into his life and work with his own auto-biography... "We have only started on our development of our country we have not as yet, with all our talk of wonderful progress, done more than scratch the surface. The progress has been wonderful enough but..."

Pages:300

Biographies/   ISBN: *1-59462-198-5*   *MSRP $21.95*

The Art of Cross-Examination
Francis Wellman

QTY

I presume it is the experience of every author, after his first book is published upon an important subject, to be almost overwhelmed with a wealth of ideas and illustrations which could readily have been included in his book, and which to his own mind, at least, seem to make a second edition inevitable. Such certainly was the case with me; and when the first edition had reached its sixth impression in five months, I rejoiced to learn that it seemed to my publishers that the book had met with a sufficiently favorable reception to justify a second and considerably enlarged edition. ..

Pages:412

Reference   **ISBN:** *1-59462-647-2*   *MSRP $19.95*

On the Duty of Civil Disobedience
Henry David Thoreau

QTY

Thoreau wrote his famous essay, On the Duty of Civil Disobedience, as a protest against an unjust but popular war and the immoral but popular institution of slave-owning. He did more than write—he declined to pay his taxes, and was hauled off to gaol in consequence. Who can say how much this refusal of his hastened the end of the war and of slavery ?

Law   **ISBN:** *1-59462-747-9*   **Pages:48**

MSRP $7.45

Dream Psychology Psychoanalysis for Beginners
Sigmund Freud

QTY

Sigmund Freud, born Sigismund Schlomo Freud (May 6, 1856 - September 23, 1939), was a Jewish-Austrian neurologist and psychiatrist who co-founded the psychoanalytic school of psychology. Freud is best known for his theories of the unconscious mind, especially involving the mechanism of repression; his redefinition of sexual desire as mobile and directed towards a wide variety of objects; and his therapeutic techniques, especially his understanding of transference in the therapeutic relationship and the presumed value of dreams as sources of insight into unconscious desires.

Pages:196

Psychology   **ISBN:** *1-59462-905-6*   *MSRP $15.45*

The Miracle of Right Thought
Orison Swett Marden

QTY

Believe with all of your heart that you will do what you were made to do. When the mind has once formed the habit of holding cheerful, happy, prosperous pictures, it will not be easy to form the opposite habit. It does not matter how improbable or how far away this realization may see, or how dark the prospects may be, if we visualize them as best we can, as vividly as possible, hold tenaciously to them and vigorously struggle to attain them, they will gradually become actualized, realized in the life. But a desire, a longing without endeavor, a yearning abandoned or held indifferently will vanish without realization.

Pages:360

Self Help   **ISBN:** *1-59462-644-8*   *MSRP $25.45*

QTY

The Rosicrucian Cosmo-Conception Mystic Christianity *by Max Heindel*   ISBN: *1-59462-188-8* **$38.95**
The Rosicrucian Cosmo-conception is not dogmatic, neither does it appeal to any other authority than the reason of the student. It is: not controversial, but is: sent forth in the, hope that it may help to clear..   New Age/Religion Pages 646

Abandonment To Divine Providence *by Jean-Pierre de Caussade*   ISBN: *1-59462-228-0* **$25.95**
"The Rev. Jean Pierre de Caussade was one of the most remarkable spiritual writers of the Society of Jesus in France in the 18th Century. His death took place at Toulouse in 1751. His works have gone through many editions and have been republished...   Inspirational/Religion Pages 400

Mental Chemistry *by Charles Haanel*   ISBN: *1-59462-192-6* **$23.95**
Mental Chemistry allows the change of material conditions by combining and appropriately utilizing the power of the mind. Much like applied chemistry creates something new and unique out of careful combinations of chemicals the mastery of mental chemistry...   New Age Pages 354

The Letters of Robert Browning and Elizabeth Barret Barrett 1845-1846 vol II   ISBN: *1-59462-193-4* **$35.95**
by Robert Browning and Elizabeth Barrett   Biographies Pages 596

Gleanings In Genesis (volume I) *by Arthur W. Pink*   ISBN: *1-59462-130-6* **$27.45**
Appropriately has Genesis been termed "the seed plot of the Bible" for in it we have, in germ form, almost all of the great doctrines which are afterwards fully developed in the books of Scripture which follow...   Religion/Inspirational Pages 420

The Master Key *by L. W. de Laurence*   ISBN: *1-59462-001-6* **$30.95**
In no branch of human knowledge has there been a more lively increase of the spirit of research during the past few years than in the study of Psychology, Concentration and Mental Discipline. The requests for authentic lessons in Thought Control, Mental Discipline and...   New Age/Business Pages 422

The Lesser Key Of Solomon Goetia *by L. W. de Laurence*   ISBN: *1-59462-092-X* **$9.95**
This translation of the first book of the "Lernegton" which is now for the first time made accessible to students of Talismanic Magic was done, after careful collation and edition, from numerous Ancient Manuscripts in Hebrew, Latin, and French...   New Age/Occult Pages 92

Rubaiyat Of Omar Khayyam *by Edward Fitzgerald*   ISBN:*1-59462-332-5* **$13.95**
Edward Fitzgerald, whom the world has already learned, in spite of his own efforts to remain within the shadow of anonymity, to look upon as one of the rarest poets of the century, was born at Bredfield, in Suffolk, on the 31st of March, 1809. He was the third son of John Purcell...   Music Pages 172

Ancient Law *by Henry Maine*   ISBN: *1-59462-128-4* **$29.95**
The chief object of the following pages is to indicate some of the earliest ideas of mankind, as they are reflected in Ancient Law, and to point out the relation of those ideas to modern thought.   Religiom/History Pages 452

Far-Away Stories *by William J. Locke*   ISBN: *1-59462-129-2* **$19.45**
"Good wine needs no bush, but a collection of mixed vintages does. And this book is just such a collection. Some of the stories I do not want to remain buried for ever in the museum files of dead magazine-numbers an author's not unpardonable vanity..."   Fiction Pages 272

Life of David Crockett *by David Crockett*   ISBN: *1-59462-250-7* **$27.45**
"Colonel David Crockett was one of the most remarkable men of the times in which he lived. Born in humble life, but gifted with a strong will, an indomitable courage, and unremitting perseverance...   Biographies/New Age Pages 424

Lip-Reading *by Edward Nitchie*   ISBN: *1-59462-206-X* **$25.95**
Edward B. Nitchie, founder of the New York School for the Hard of Hearing, now the Nitchie School of Lip-Reading, Inc, wrote "LIP-READING Principles and Practice". The development and perfecting of this meritorious work on lip-reading was an undertaking...   How-to Pages 400

A Handbook of Suggestive Therapeutics, Applied Hypnotism, Psychic Science   ISBN: *1-59462-214-0* **$24.95**
by Henry Munro   Health/New Age/Health/Self-help Pages 376

A Doll's House: and Two Other Plays *by Henrik Ibsen*   ISBN: *1-59462-112-8* **$19.95**
Henrik Ibsen created this classic when in revolutionary 1848 Rome. Introducing some striking concepts in playwriting for the realist genre, this play has been studied the world over.   Fiction/Classics/Plays 308

The Light of Asia *by sir Edwin Arnold*   ISBN: *1-59462-204-3* **$13.95**
In this poetic masterpiece, Edwin Arnold describes the life and teachings of Buddha. The man who was to become known as Buddha to the world was born as Prince Gautama of India but he rejected the worldly riches and abandoned the reigns of power when...   Religion/History/Biographies Pages 170

The Complete Works of Guy de Maupassant *by Guy de Maupassant*   ISBN: *1-59462-157-8* **$16.95**
"For days and days, nights and nights, I had dreamed of that first kiss which was to consecrate our engagement, and I knew not on what spot I should put my lips..."   Fiction/Classics Pages 240

The Art of Cross-Examination *by Francis L. Wellman*   ISBN: *1-59462-309-0* **$26.95**
Written by a renowned trial lawyer, Wellman imparts his experience and uses case studies to explain how to use psychology to extract desired information through questioning.   How-to/Science/Reference Pages 408

Answered or Unanswered? *by Louisa Vaughan*   ISBN: *1-59462-248-5* **$10.95**
Miracles of Faith in China   Religion Pages 112

The Edinburgh Lectures on Mental Science (1909) *by Thomas*   ISBN: *1-59462-008-3* **$11.95**
This book contains the substance of a course of lectures recently given by the writer in the Queen Street Hail, Edinburgh. Its purpose is to indicate the Natural Principles governing the relation between Mental Action and Material Conditions...   New Age/Psychology Pages 148

Ayesha *by H. Rider Haggard*   ISBN: *1-59462-301-5* **$24.95**
Verily and indeed it is the unexpected that happens! Probably if there was one person upon the earth from whom the Editor of this, and of a certain previous history, did not expect to hear again...   Classics Pages 380

Ayala's Angel *by Anthony Trollope*   ISBN: *1-59462-352-X* **$29.95**
The two girls were both pretty, but Lucy who was twenty-one who supposed to be simple and comparatively unattractive, whereas Ayala was credited, as her Bombwhat romantic name might show, with poetic charm and a taste for romance, Ayala when her father died was nineteen...   Fiction Pages 484

The American Commonwealth *by James Bryce*   ISBN: *1-59462-286-8* **$34.45**
An interpretation of American democratic political theory. It examines political mechanics and society from the perspective of Scotsman James Bryce   Politics Pages 572

Stories of the Pilgrims *by Margaret P. Pumphrey*   ISBN: *1-59462-116-0* **$17.95**
This book explores pilgrims religious oppression in England as well as their escape to Holland and eventual crossing to America on the Mayflower, and their early days in New England...   History Pages 268

QTY

The Fasting Cure *by Sinclair Upton*   ISBN: 1-59462-222-1 $13.95
In the Cosmopolitan Magazine for May, 1910, and in the Contemporary Review (London) for April, 1910, I published an article dealing with my experiences in fasting. I have written a great many magazine articles, but never one which attracted so much attention... New Age/Self Help/Health Pages 164

Hebrew Astrology *by Sepharial*   ISBN: 1-59462-308-2 $13.45
In these days of advanced thinking it is a matter of common observation that we have left many of the old landmarks behind and that we are now pressing forward to greater heights and to a wider horizon than that which represented the mind-content of our progenitors... Astrology Pages 144

Thought Vibration or The Law of Attraction in the Thought World   ISBN: 1-59462-127-6 $12.95

by William Walker Atkinson   Psychology/Religion Pages 144

Optimism *by Helen Keller*   ISBN: 1-59462-108-X $15.95
Helen Keller was blind, deaf, and mute since 19 months old, yet famously learned how to overcome these handicaps, communicate with the world, and spread her lectures promoting optimism. An inspiring read for everyone... Biographies/Inspirational Pages 84

Sara Crewe *by Frances Burnett*   ISBN: 1-59462-360-0 $9.45
In the first place, Miss Minchin lived in London. Her home was a large, dull, tall one, in a large, dull square, where all the houses were alike, and all the sparrows were alike, and where all the door-knockers made the same heavy sound... Childrens/Classic Pages 88

The Autobiography of Benjamin Franklin *by Benjamin Franklin*   ISBN: 1-59462-135-7 $24.95
The Autobiography of Benjamin Franklin has probably been more extensively read than any other American historical work, and no other book of its kind has had such ups and downs of fortune. Franklin lived for many years in England, where he was agent... Biographies/History Pages 332

Name	
Email	
Telephone	
Address	
City, State ZIP	

☐ **Credit Card**   ☐ **Check / Money Order**

Credit Card Number	
Expiration Date	
Signature	

Please Mail to: Book Jungle
PO Box 2226
Champaign, IL 61825
or Fax to: 630-214-0564

www.ingramcontent.com/pod-product-compliance
Lightning Source LLC
Chambersburg PA
CBHW080824020726
47501CB00009B/2408